DAREDEVIL AMY

"Last one in is a—Hey, Amy!" Stevie shouted. Everybody turned to look. Amy had climbed to a rocky edge five feet above the water and was flexing her knees and swinging her arms.

"No diving!" John called out.

Amy grinned mischievously. She crossed her heart, just as she had when promising Eli she wouldn't dive and, without further ado, she jumped off the rock, tipped forward, touched her toes, straightened out, and dove straight into the water.

"Amy!" Seth shrieked.

Nobody else spoke or moved. They waited. Although the water was clear, the sun sparkled on it, making it difficult to see below the surface. There was no sign of Amy. . . .

THE SADDLE CLUB

PACK TRIP

BONNIE BRYANT

A BANTAM SKYLARK BOOK®
NEW YORK · TORONTO · LONDON · SYDNEY · AUCKLAND

RL 5, 009–012

PACK TRIP
A Bantam Skylark Book / October 1991

ISBN 0-553-15928-3

Published simultaneously in the United States and Canada

PRINTED IN THE UNITED STATES OF AMERICA

CWO   0 9 8 7 6 5 4 3 2 1

PACK
TRIP

1

CAROLE HANSON LOOKED around at the walls of her bedroom. She was convinced that there must be enough space for just one more horse poster. She had a new one that showed a championship horse in the middle of a jump at an international event. The rider's position was just perfect. Carole was sure that if she studied the position at the same time that she admired the beauty of the horse, she could really learn something. After all, she had learned something from all of her other posters. She'd learned that she was absolutely crazy about horses.

Every inch of every wall in Carole's room was covered with pictures of horses and riders. The door to her closet had a chart of horse colors and breeds. The inside of the closet door had a poster of English riding tack. Practically the only thing that wasn't covered with horse pictures was her window. Carole cocked her head and studied the poster and the problem. Then she smiled. She had the perfect solution.

"Bingo!" she said. Maybe she couldn't put her poster on the window, but she *could* put it on the window shade. That way she could just roll it down whenever she wanted to look at it.

She shuffled through the mess she thought of as her desk to find some tape, and within a few minutes the new poster was up. She was pleased to realize that she actually still had room for yet another—a small one—on the shade. Satisfied, she sat on her bed to admire her handiwork. She couldn't wait to tell her best friends, Stevie Lake and Lisa Atwood, what she'd done. They would want to see the poster, too.

Stevie, Lisa, and Carole were three very different girls, but they had one very important thing in common. They were all crazy about horses. Carole was the best rider of the three, having been raised on Marine Corps bases where her father, a colonel, was stationed. She had started riding when she was very young, and though she couldn't make up her mind what she wanted to be when she grew up, she joked that she had narrowed her choices down to three things: horses, horses, and horses.

Carole had her own horse, a bay gelding with a perfect star on his face. His name was Starlight, and he was just about the most important thing in her life. Starlight boarded at Pine Hollow Stables, where Lisa and Stevie also rode and took lessons.

The three girls were all so horse crazy that they had formed their own club, The Saddle Club. It had only two rules: Members had to be horse crazy, and they had to be willing to help one another out. The first part was easy. The second part was harder and sometimes got them into trouble, especially when Stevie, who could be a mischievous practical joker, was in charge. Carole and Lisa didn't usually mind, though. Being with Stevie was sometimes trouble, but it was almost always fun.

Lisa was more serious than her friends. She was a straight-A student who approached problems systematically and analytically. In contrast, Carole could sometimes be a little flaky, unless the problem concerned horses, in which case she was all business.

Together the threesome made a great team. As The Saddle Club they'd accomplished an awful lot. Carole sometimes wondered what more they would accomplish in the future. There was no way of telling, of course, but she was confident that the team of three was a lot more powerful than just the three individuals who made up the group.

Carole laced her fingers behind her head and leaned back against her pillow. Her eyes focused on the ceiling of her room. It was all white. There was nothing on it.

"Oh!" she said, sitting up abruptly. Her ceiling was the perfect place to put her rodeo and Western posters!

One of Carole's father's friends, Frank Devine, had two things that made him wonderful in Carole's eyes. First of all, he had a dude ranch where The Saddle Club had been able to expand their horsemanship beyond the English riding they usually did at Pine Hollow. Second, he had a daughter who was just a little bit older than Carole, Lisa, and Stevie. Kate Devine had been an international competitor in English riding events before her father bought the dude ranch. Now Kate was very content to exchange her riding crop and hard hat for spurs and a cowboy hat. The Saddle Club had visited the Devine's ranch, the Bar-None, twice and found that Western riding was lots of fun, too. In fact, they liked it, and Kate, so much, that they had invited Kate and her friend, Christine Lonetree, to join The Saddle Club as out-of-town members. Carole's only regret was that she didn't get to see as much of Kate and Christine as she would have liked.

Carole bounded off her bed. Now that she'd figured out where to hang the Western and rodeo posters, she didn't want to waste a second. The only problem was that it was going to take more than a second to remember where she had put them.

She opened her closet door and shuffled through the papers on the lower shelf. She found the original copy of her science report from two years ago accompanied by a chart of the food chain, but there was no sign of the collection of rodeo posters. She moved her desk chair over to the closet and climbed onto it so she could reach the top shelf.

It had a lot of interesting things on it. There was an Easter hat she had worn when she was seven, her Brownie uniform from the troop she had joined when she lived in California, a half-finished needlepoint of a horse (she had stopped working on it because the horse's proportions were all wrong), and a bottle of after-shave lotion she had bought for her father for Christmas. She'd hidden it so well, even *she* couldn't find it!

She was so involved in her rummaging that she didn't hear her father knock and enter her room. "If you're trying to run away from home, the front door is more efficient," her father teased. Carole was so startled that she bumped her head on the closet doorjamb. Dazed, she lowered herself from the upper reaches of her closet.

"Merry Christmas," she said, handing him the aftershave lotion. She rubbed her head where she'd hit it.

"Thank you, dear," he said. He offered to kiss the growing bump on her head. She let him do it. They knew it wouldn't keep her from getting a bruise, but it made them both feel better. "I didn't mean to startle you," he said. "I just wanted to let you know there's a phone call for you."

"For me? Who is it?"

"Oh, just someone named something like Kit, no, maybe Kat—something about a dude ranch . . ."

"Kate!" she said, bounding off the chair and toward the telephone. "Why didn't you tell me?"

Colonel Hanson laughed. "I tried," he said.

Carole picked up the phone. "Hi! How are you? What's new? Are you coming for a visit?"

"It's so nice to hear your voice, Carole," Kate said, laughing at the jumble of questions Carole had just thrown at her.

Carole sat down and took a deep breath. She told Kate she had just been thinking about her because of the rodeo posters. "I can't find them, and it's really bothering me."

"You mean those posters you put under your bed for safekeeping?" Kate asked.

"Yes, those," Carole said. "Now where do you suppose they could be?"

"Under your bed?" Kate repeated.

Then it dawned on Carole. That was just where they were. "You knew exactly when to call. You're a perfect friend!" Carole said.

"I'm better than that," Kate said. "I'm a perfect friend who's got good connections in the horse world."

Carole was suddenly alert. She had the funniest feeling that something wonderful was coming. "Yes?" she said expectantly. "What is it?"

"Remember Eli?"

Of course Carole did. Kate was just teasing her. Eli had been the main ranch hand at the Bar None. Now he was a college student, studying rodeo riding and working for the Bar None when they needed an extra hand.

"Well, Eli's come up with an idea," Kate continued. "He'd like to take some young riders on a mountain pack trip. Naturally he wants only the best riders. Naturally he asked if I could go, and Christine, too. Naturally when we said we could, he wanted to know if we knew any other good riders. We weren't sure—"

"You mean it?" Carole interrupted.

"Of course I do," Kate said. "It's going to be a five-day trip. We'll bring some of the horses from the Bar None to use, and Jeannie is coming along, too."

Jeannie was Eli's girlfriend and another person The Saddle Club really liked. They took more than a little credit for the fact that Eli had ever noticed Jeannie was alive. It would be great to spend time with her, too.

"I'll be there. I'll be there. When is it?" Carole asked.

"Week after next. My dad already talked to yours, and they've got it all arranged. But here's the big question. Do you think Stevie and Lisa want to come, too?"

"That's the easiest question in the world to answer," Carole said. "Of course they *want* to come. The question is *can* they? I mean, is it really expensive?"

"Not too bad, but your dad said something to me about using the money some banker gave you."

There were so many nice thoughts filling Carole's head that for a minute she couldn't remember what her father had been talking about. Then it came to her.

"Veronica's horse!" she said.

"Huh?" Kate asked.

"It was a reward. The Saddle Club saved Veronica diAngelo's horse from horsenappers, and her father gave us a reward."

"Why would you take money from him?" Kate asked. It was a good question. Veronica diAngelo was the snobbiest girl at Pine Hollow, and The Saddle Club never wanted to have anything to do with her. That didn't mean they would let her horse be stolen, though. They cared about her horse even if they didn't care much about her.

"Oh, we didn't really want the money," Carole explained. "We just took it because we knew it would make Veronica angry. But now I'm glad we took it, because it means we can all go on the trip with you and Eli."

"I hope so," Kate said.

"Definitely," Carole assured her. "I think," she added.

"Call me," Kate said.

"As soon as I can," Carole promised.

STEVIE TURNED ANOTHER page of *Robinson Crusoe*, satisfied that she was making progress in her book-report book. The trouble was that she didn't have the foggiest idea what had happened on the page she'd just turned.

She was going to flip back a page, but her cat, Madonna, eased herself in front of Stevie and settled down on the open book, closing the subject for the moment. Stevie began patting her since it was clear that was what the cat had in mind.

"Stevie, phone for you," her older brother, Chad, announced. "It's Carole. Don't take all night. I'm waiting for a call from Belinda."

"Sure," Stevie said agreeably, though she didn't mean it at all. She didn't like Belinda. She *did* like Carole.

"What's up?" she asked brightly, tucking the phone comfortably between her shoulder and her ear so she could continue to pat Madonna as she talked.

"Kate Devine called," Carole began. All thoughts of the poor stranded Mr. Crusoe fled from Stevie's mind. She began patting Madonna so vigorously that the cat slunk away, regarding Stevie curiously as she went. Any time Kate Devine called, it was at the very least interesting and more likely exciting.

Stevie listened intently while Carole explained about the trip. It sounded almost too good to be true, especially when Carole described how Kate's father, a retired Marine Corps pilot with access to an airplane, would fly the three of them out west for free. That way all they would have to pay for was the cost of the pack trip itself.

"That's all? Hey, great, but how are we going to manage that?" Stevie asked.

"Mr. diAngelo's reward money," Carole said.

"Ahhhh! Perfect!" Stevie said. "It's just what we had in mind, isn't it? First, we irk her by getting the money from her father, then we drive her crazy by doing something absolutely wonderful with it. Carole, you're a genius!"

It took them another twenty minutes to talk about

how great the trip was going to be. Chad came into Stevie's room three times to glare at her for tying up the phone. She didn't pay much attention to him until he reminded her that her own boyfriend, Phil, might be trying to call. Stevie glared back.

"I've got to go," she told Carole. "Chad is trying some awful tactics to get me off the phone, and I don't want him to think they're working, but the fact is I've got to tell my parents about this. They're going to be thrilled. I'll call you back as soon as I can, okay?"

"Deal," Carole said. "In the meantime I'll call Lisa."

LISA WAS RELIEVED when the telephone rang. She was bored with her parents' tedious discussion. They were in the process of planning an anniversary trip for themselves, and at the moment they were trying to decide where Lisa would stay while they were gone. Her brother was studying in Europe, so he wouldn't be available to look after her. As far as Lisa was concerned, it was an easy question. She'd stay with Stevie or Carole, or both. For her parents, however, that kind of question was never easy. Her mother was at the point where she was worrying about how many suitcases Lisa would need and whether they should tell the police the house would be empty during their vacation. Lisa much preferred answering the telephone rather than continuing the conversation. She decided that if the caller turned out to be a magazine salesperson, she'd order a five-year subscription to *Golf Digest* just to pay her parents back for being so boring.

It wasn't a magazine salesperson. It was Carole. And within a few seconds, Lisa realized, it was also the answer to her prayers—several of them.

"You're kidding! A pack trip! Week after next? Wait until I tell my parents!"

"Will they give you a hard time?" Carole asked.

"Not at all. They'll be thrilled," Lisa said. She explained about her parents' trip. "Of course, they'll load me down with phone numbers and fax numbers where they can be reached while they're away."

"Fax numbers?" Carole asked.

"In case they have to sign any consent forms," Lisa explained. "These people never leave anything to chance!"

Carole laughed. "That's okay," she said. "As long as they say yes."

"I'll call you back," Lisa promised.

"JUST EXACTLY WHAT does 'no' mean?" Stevie asked her parents patiently.

"It's an adverb," her father answered just as patiently.

"It means the opposite of 'yes.' It means you've got a book report to do, and you have to keep up-to-date on your journal, and going on a wild-goose chase—"

"It's a pack trip," Stevie corrected him.

"Same thing," he said. "In any event, there are things that haven't been getting done which must get done, and you know that schoolwork always comes before horses . . ."

Stevie had her work cut out for her. She could tell there was major resistance from her parents. Convincing them to let her go was going to take time and diplomacy.

". . . so the answer is no."

"Why don't I get us all something to drink while we continue this discussion?" Stevie suggested. "Sodas?"

Stevie was not above bribery at any level. Besides, she told herself, it was a way of proving how responsible she was.

"Continue? I thought it was over," her father said.

"Don't interrupt her now, dear," Mrs. Lake said. "She hasn't gotten to the really creative part yet, and that's always fun."

Stevie's parents knew her well, but she also knew them. She was convinced she could make them change their minds. It would just take time.

"WE'RE ALL COMING, Kate, and I can't believe it!" Carole

practically screeched into the telephone. "It's going to be The Saddle Club's biggest adventure yet. We can't wait!"

"Did Lisa and Stevie have any problems convincing their parents?" Kate asked.

"Lisa didn't, but Stevie took a long time," Carole said. "See, she has a book report she has to do, and she's supposed to be keeping a journal. She had to promise her parents that she'd finish reading the book and do the first draft of the book report before she got home."

"What's the book?"

"*Robinson Crusoe*," Carole said. "It's about this guy who gets stranded on an island."

"I can help her with that, because I've already read it," Kate said. "Isn't that what Saddle Clubbers are supposed to do—help one another?"

"Precisely," Carole said. "And since she's now on page four of the book, we'll have lots of opportunities to help. Isn't that wonderful?"

"We'll be reading by firelight," Kate said.

"Just like Abraham Lincoln," Carole remarked. It made Stevie's homework sound more exciting than Carole suspected it would be.

"But the important thing is that you're all coming!"

"Yes. So, what do we have to bring?"

It seemed to Carole that there were a million things to

consider. First of all, since it would be cold at night, Kate suggested that they borrow some Marine Corps subzero sleeping bags.

"It won't be subzero, will it?" Carole asked.

"Probably not, but it can get pretty cold in the mountains," Kate said. "On that score better safe than sorry."

Carole made a note to ask her father for the sleeping bags.

They discussed everything from shirts and sweatshirts to combs and brushes. They were about to decide which person should bring the toothpaste that they could all use ("Not Stevie. She brought bubble–gum–flavored toothpaste to riding camp!") when Carole's father reminded her that somebody—specifically he—was going to have to pay for the phone call.

"Dad, we haven't even gotten to the blankets, buckets, grooming gear, and tack for the horses!" Carole complained.

"Let the horses pack for themselves," he suggested drily. "After all, aren't they packhorses?"

"Very funny," Carole said sarcastically. She managed to hold her giggle until her father had left the room. She certainly didn't want him to know she actually thought his joke was funny.

"I've got to go, but guess what my dad just said. . . ."

When Carole and Kate finally hung up a few minutes later, it was almost bedtime. Carole went downstairs to where her father was watching the news and gave him a big hug.

"Excited, honey?" he asked.

She just nodded. She was too excited even to try to describe how excited she was.

"I'm sure you'll all have a great time."

She gave him another hug. "See you in the morning."

"Okay," he agreed. "Then we can talk about what to pack for the horses if you really don't think they're up to it themselves."

She laughed and headed back upstairs.

Before she went to sleep, she took out her Western and rodeo posters and looked them over carefully. She told herself she was just trying to decide which she would put where on the ceiling of her room, but she knew differently. She knew she was looking at them to remind herself how much she loved Western riding and how much she was going to enjoy the pack trip. Finally, realizing that she didn't need much reminding on those subjects, she slid the posters back under her bed and turned out the light.

She pulled the blankets up high to protect herself from the subzero temperatures in her imagination.

3

"FASTEN YOUR SEAT belts, girls," Frank Devine said from the pilot's seat.

"Aye, aye, sir," Carole joked, though the reminder was totally unnecessary since The Saddle Club knew perfectly well that Frank was about to land the plane. They could even see the airport below them.

"In fifteen minutes we'll be starting our pack trip!" Lisa said excitedly.

"We have a two-hour drive before our pack trip begins," Stevie reminded her.

"Well, you know what I mean."

"What she means is that in fifteen minutes, we'll be

getting into a car pulling a horse trailer and beginning a two-hour Saddle Club meeting," Carole said.

"Haven't you just had a three-and-a-half-hour Saddle Club meeting?" Frank asked. "The three of you have talked about nothing but horses since we left Washington."

"That's not true," Stevie said. "We also talked about my boyfriend, Phil."

"Who rides horses," Frank added.

The four of them laughed. It was true, but it always seemed that there could never be too much time to talk about horses.

Frank received his final clearance from the tower at the airport and brought the plane down for a smooth landing. The girls clapped, and he smiled in acknowledgment.

"My pleasure," he said. "It's always fun to ferry you three around. Otherwise, how else am I going to keep up on the gossip around Pine Hollow?"

Following the directions of a man wearing earphones and holding yellow flashlights, Frank drew the plane to a gentle halt. The engine slowed and then silenced. They had arrived. The pack trip was about to begin.

It took a while to unload all of the gear from the plane. As usual Lisa's mother had packed Lisa's bags as if she were going around the world, instead of just around a mountain. Lisa had managed to talk her out of packing her off-the-shoulder cotton evening dress, panty hose, and high-heeled sandals. She hadn't been able to talk her mother out of packing what her mother called an après sun robe. Lisa had, however, managed to remove it and hide it under a chair in her room before she left for the airport. Even her best friends might not have understood that one!

"I can't believe it! We're almost on our way!" Stevie shouted, dropping her duffel bag so she could hug Kate and Christine at the same time.

Mel, Eli's dog and Stevie's old friend, wagged her tail briskly. She jumped up on the threesome, and willing hands brought her in on the hug, too. Lisa and Carole joined in.

"Are we going to hug, or are we going to ride?" Eli asked pointedly after a moment.

"Both!" several voices answered simultaneously.

"But let's get moving first," Carole suggested.

IT TOOK A while to finish unloading the luggage, stow it in the van with the horse gear, confirm meeting points, say good-bye to Frank, and reassure everybody about emergency phone numbers.

"Now remember, be careful out there, Eli," Frank said. "That's real wilderness."

Kate turned to her father and put her hands on her hips. "When you start reminding Eli about things he already knows, it's definitely time to go, Dad," Kate said.

He gave her a final hug. "Have fun," he said.

"That's more like it," she said, returning his hug.

The first thing they did after the luggage was packed was to make sure the horses were comfortable. The trailers had enough horses for all the Saddle Club girls. Eli, Jeannie, and the other riders would use local horses. The packhorses were going to be local mounts, too.

The girls had each been assigned a horse from the Bar None's herd on their first day at the ranch. Eli had done the assigning, and each of the girls thought she'd gotten a perfect horse.

Carole greeted her strawberry roan, named Berry, with a big hug. She gave him a lump of sugar.

"This came all the way from the coffee shop in the airport in Washington!" she told the horse. He seemed unimpressed by that but pleased to see her nevertheless.

Lisa's horse was a bay mare named Chocolate. Seeing Chocolate made Lisa recall all the good times they'd had together. They had gone on a roundup and on a sunrise ride. They had even competed in a rodeo. She wished she'd brought Chocolate some sugar the way Carole had remembered to do for Berry. Chocolate didn't seem to be jealous, though.

Stevie stepped into the little stall on the trailer holding her horse. He was a brown-and-white pinto—a coloration usually called skewbald. His name was Stewball, and it suited him perfectly. The color blotches made him look very odd, but that wasn't the reason. It was because he was the fastest, cleverest horse Stevie had ever known. When Stevie had had a race against Eli, it was Stewball, not Stevie, who had figured out how to take a shortcut and win.

Stevie flung her arms around the horse's neck and buried her face in his soft mane.

"Together again at last!" she announced. The horse regarded her skeptically. She laughed. One of the reasons she really loved Stewball was that she thought he was as funny as she was. She patted him affectionately. Then she checked his water and hay. When she was satisfied that he'd be fine until they reached their rendezvous point, she joined her friends in the back of the station wagon.

"Well, what shall we talk about?" Stevie asked, settling in.

"Horses!" came four replies, simultaneously.

"Tell us about how you all saved Veronica's horse from horsenappers," Christine said. "What happened?"

There was so much to tell! When they'd finished that story, the girls started in on the latest happenings at the Bar None. The last time they'd visited, the dude ranch had been suffering from a drop in customers. Kate assured the eastern visitors that the ranch was now thriving, thanks in part to their help. The five girls had participated in the local rodeo, drawing a lot of good attention to the ranch.

"We've been full now almost all summer. Isn't it wonderful?" Kate asked.

"Sure, as long as there's room for us when we want to come visit," Lisa said.

"Anytime," Kate assured her.

Although two hours had sounded like a long drive, there was so much to talk about that the time flew. When they finished catching up on what had happened, they talked about what was going to happen.

"You know, I said yes so fast for this trip that I forgot to ask where we're going," Stevie said.

"We're going round a mountain," Christine said.

"No, we're going *up* a mountain," Kate told her. "We're going to start out in a pass between some mountains—"

She rifled through some papers in an envelope and pulled out a map.

"Here we go," she said, pointing out the route. "We'll be here in this pass, which is like a valley—"

"Look! Lakes," Stevie said.

"And they're all named after you," Christine quipped.

"I've heard it before," Stevie told her.

"I'm sorry," Christine said. "Nobody whose last name is Lonetree should make jokes about someone whose last name is Lake."

"Deal," Stevie said.

"Anyway," Kate continued. "We'll be spending two days and two nights in the mountain pass before we take the trail up around the mountain. Eli said we have to make it the full way up and down the mountain before nightfall, because it's too cold up there—and we will go above the timberline—to spend the night with a bunch of, and I quote here, 'greenhorn dudes.'"

The girls giggled. Calling them greenhorn dudes sounded just like Eli, even though they knew he respected their knowledge of horses and their riding ability.

"The whole trip will take five days. Eli says we'll be in all different kinds of terrain, everything from lush prairie to rocky trails."

"It's going to be wonderful!" Lisa declared, sighing contentedly in anticipation.

"What do we know about the other kids who are coming on the trip?" Carole asked.

Kate shrugged.

"Not much," Christine said. "Two boys and a girl. One of the boys is the girl's brother. They're about our age. They live north of here."

Lisa thought that could be interesting. She wondered what the boys would be like. Stevie had a boyfriend, but Carole and Lisa didn't. It didn't bother Lisa, since she had never been particularly interested in anybody. Now, however, she found herself intrigued by the idea that there would be two boys along. What if one of them was really cute and fun? Her mind filled with images of riding side by side on mountain trails edged with lush ponderosa pines. She could see the breathtaking mountain scenery and smell the fresh, cool air. She could almost feel the joy of sharing it all with someone special.

"*Won't* you, Lisa?" Carole said pointedly. Carole was obviously repeating the question, but Lisa had been daydreaming and had no idea what the question was.

"Huh?" She blushed a little.

"I said you're so smart, you'll figure out how to follow the instructions to pitch our tents."

"Not if she's daydreaming like that!" Stevie joked.

"Sorry. I was just daydreaming about how beautiful the scenery is going to be."

"That's funny," Stevie said. "I got the impression you started daydreaming when Christine told us there would be two boys along on the trip."

"Like I care," Lisa said, but she was beginning to get the feeling that she did.

THE VANS PULLED to a halt next to a wooden cabin surrounded by corrals. It was Eli's friend's house, where they and the horses were to spend the night before their dawn departure the next day. It took only a few minutes to unload the horses and see to their needs.

"I bet they're awfully happy to be on firm ground," Lisa said.

The horses seemed to agree. They proceeded into the corral slowly, alert for anything that might be different about this new, if temporary, home. Lisa laughed watching Chocolate. The horse sniffed around, stepping cautiously, just the way Lisa's dog did when he was in a new place. Stewball, on the other hand, bounded out of the trailer and into the corral. He circled it twice, checking out every inch of it at near breakneck speed, and then drew to a sudden halt in front of the water.

"You knew what you were doing when you picked Stewball for me, didn't you, Eli?" Stevie teased.

Eli ignored the question. "Fresh hay is in the barn," he told the girls. "Grain is in the vans."

"He's just like Max," Stevie said to Kate. "Whatever else is going on, the horses come first."

Kate nodded in agreement. But there was no arguing. After all, horses *did* come first. "Let's get a bale of hay," she said. The two of them headed for the barn.

When they returned, they found that another car had pulled up next to the vans. The other riders had arrived. Stevie and Kate joined their friends for the introductions.

The brother and sister were named Seth and Amy. At first Stevie was struck by how much they looked alike, with their smooth dark brown hair and eyes to match. But very quickly she sensed their differences. Seth seemed to hold back, almost shyly, while Amy bounced around, shaking everybody's hand. Her dark eyes flashed with excitement. "I can't wait to start tomorrow!" she declared loudly. "It seems like we've had months of preparation for this, and all we've been doing is riding on the dumb old trail right near our barn. This is going to be *wild!*"

Stevie thought the girl's words summed up her own thoughts exactly. Amy was going to be fun.

"Take it easy, Amy," Seth said. "We don't want it to be too wild, do we?"

"Says who?" Amy challenged.

Stevie laughed. Then she saw the third new arrival. "Hi, I'm Stevie," she said, offering her hand.

"I'm John." He shook her hand, but his eyes went beyond her to the corral. "Does anybody know which is my horse?" he asked.

"I do," Carole said. "I'll show you." It was hard for Carole to understand somebody whose first thought of an overnight trail ride was that it was "wild," but it was easy for her to understand somebody whose first thought was about his own horse. She had a feeling that she and John would get along just fine.

Lisa blushed when she realized that she'd been staring at Seth, and she hoped nobody had noticed. She thought she was safe. Everybody, including Seth, seemed to be watching Amy, who was doing a very good job of imitating a horse that didn't want to get off a trailer.

"So I stood behind him and made a sound like a carrot!" she said. "Worked like a dream!" Everybody laughed, including Seth. Lisa laughed, too.

This was going to be a wonderful trip, she was sure.

4

When the last of the duffel bags were stowed on the pack saddles, it was time to go.

Eli had gotten the riders out of their sleeping bags before dawn. Now it was still early, and the morning fog clung to the hillsides, masking the trail.

"It's so mysterious," Lisa said to Carole. "Will the horses mind the fog?"

"I don't think so," she said. "Besides, it won't be foggy for long. Within the hour the sun will be so bright, we'll be peeling off our layers of clothes and wishing it would cool down."

"Which it will. By tonight, higher up in the pass, it will be so cold, you won't believe it!" Kate told her.

"Mountain trips are like that, with big temperature swings."

"I know. I'm prepared. I just hope the horses are," Lisa said.

"Mount up and let's get moving!" Eli called out, interrupting the chatter. The riders were only too eager to obey.

Lisa patted Chocolate warmly on the neck, took the reins in her left hand, and hoisted herself into the saddle. Eli helped her adjust the stirrups. It always took her a few minutes to get used to the fact that the stirrups were lower in Western riding than in English. It was one of the few differences that she noticed at all. She soon felt right at home on board Chocolate, and she was excited about spending most of the next five days there.

On signal from Eli, the riders and the packhorses formed a single line and started off. Lisa noticed that nobody was talking, and she wondered why. It wasn't because of the difficulty of the trail. In fact, they were riding along the side of a road. For the moment, anyway, the path was quite straight and flat—no challenge at all. Perhaps, Lisa thought, it was because of the early hour and the chill of the morning. Lisa glanced at her watch. It was about eight o'clock, and they had been up since five-thirty. But Eli had shooed them into bed by nine-thirty, so they'd all had enough sleep; that wasn't it. So why weren't they talking?

She looked around, but what she noticed wasn't the other riders. It was the strange new world around her. It was what everybody else was noticing, too, and she soon realized that it was why nobody was talking.

The road they were following threaded its way between two mountains. At this hour they were still partially enshrouded by the morning fog, which now hovered about halfway up the fir trees that edged the road to the right. To the left was a field, filled with bright wildflowers and dotted with occasional evergreens. Beyond the field was the sheer cliff of a mountain, rising dramatically skyward into the dense fog.

"Oh!" Lisa gasped, noticing it all for the first time.

"Something, isn't it?" a voice behind her said.

She turned in the saddle, pleased to see that the speaker was Seth, Amy's attractive brother. She nodded.

A breeze came through, shifting the fog around like curtains. At one moment she could see mountains beyond, at the next they were completely hidden.

Chocolate paused to munch on a dandelion. Lisa tugged firmly at her bridle. It wasn't that the dandelion was bad for the horse or that she didn't want her to have a snack. It was just a bad idea to let a horse do anything without permission. She'd seen too many riders get into trouble by letting their horses take the lead. Chocolate obeyed Lisa's signal and continued along the roadway.

Fifteen minutes later the fog was gone. It had disappeared almost magically, rising to reveal the incredibly beautiful landscape that surrounded the riders and their horses.

"Up ahead we're going to leave the road," Eli called back to the riders. "We'll be in an open field, and we're going to trot for a bit to let the horses stretch."

Lisa could see where they were going to turn. They were going left, directly toward the sheer cliff. The trail through the field led to a side of the mountain where, Lisa presumed, there was a trail that circled it. Eli gave the signal, and the riders left the road, entering the field.

"Now we're really beginning our trip," Stevie said.

"You don't count the first two thousand miles we covered in an airplane?" Carole teased.

"You know what I mean," Stevie said.

"Yes, I do. And you're right," Carole conceded.

"Ready to trot?" Eli called back. All of the riders nodded. As soon as Eli's horse picked up the pace, the other horses joined in.

Lisa loved to trot. It had always been her favorite gait. It was fast enough to be exciting and slow enough to be safe. In English riding the riders usually posted when their horses trotted. In Western, the riders normally just sat the trot. There was no rule against posting in Western, but it wasn't the way it was done. When Chocolate trotted, Lisa never even thought about posting. The mare had a wonderfully smooth trot, and Lisa had no trouble sitting it out.

She was so involved in admiring Chocolate's trot that it took her a moment to notice the thumping sound of another horse bearing down on her and Chocolate. Lisa looked over her shoulder. It was Amy, and her horse wasn't trotting. Amy had gotten her horse to canter, only in Western riding that faster three-beat gait was called a lope. Amy had a big grin on her face, and it didn't change when Jeannie called out after her, telling her to bring her horse back to a trot.

"You're supposed to trot!" Lisa called to Amy, thinking that she might not have heard Jeannie's warning. "Tighten up on the reins, sit deep in the saddle. He'll slow down," Lisa said.

Amy glanced at her, barely acknowledging Lisa's presence as she passed by.

Almost instantly Jeannie came by at a gallop. When her horse was next to Amy's, she reached out, grabbed the reins, and drew the horse to a stop. By then Eli had figured out that something was going on, and he brought all of the riders to a halt.

"Are you okay?" Jeannie asked Amy.

"Of course," Amy retorted. "Why shouldn't I be?"

"Your horse was out of control," Jeannie said.

"Out of *your* control, maybe," Amy said tartly. "He was doing just what I told him to."

"But it wasn't what *I* told him," Eli said, stepping in.

"Who's riding him, you or me?" Amy challenged.

Lisa gasped. She couldn't imagine talking back to Eli that way.

"Amy!" Seth said. "Remember, you're not supposed to do that kind of thing. Eli's in charge." He turned to Eli. "I'm sorry," he said. "She just forgets sometimes. Don't worry, okay? I won't let it happen again."

Eli looked quizzically at Seth and seemed to be about to say something. He changed his mind, though, and just nodded. "Okay, let's get going again, at a *trot* until we reach the wooded trail. Ready?"

They were ready, and the trail ride continued.

When they came back down to a walk, Eli had them ride side by side. Lisa was pleased to find herself next to Seth.

"You're a good rider," Seth said to her. "Have you been riding long?"

"Not really," she said. "It's just that I love it so much that I do a lot of it, especially with my friends. I guess I've learned a lot in a short time. Do you ride a lot, too?"

"Pretty much," he said. "Amy and I ride at my mother's place. She's got a stableful of horses, so whenever we're there, we get to ride as much as we want."

"It must be wonderful having horses right there. You don't even have to drive to a stable, and they're all *your* horses," Lisa said. "I mean, my parents say I spend so much time at Pine Hollow that I might as well live there, but it's not the same, is it? You're lucky to be able to just finish your breakfast and walk out to the barn. That's the way it is with Kate, who lives on a dude ranch, and Christine, who has her own horse. Carole has a horse of her own, too. His name is Starlight. He lives at Pine Hollow, though, and on weekends she has to take a bus to the stable. On weekdays, of course, she can walk from school, but . . ."

Lisa had the funny feeling that what she was saying wasn't making much sense, but she didn't seem to be able to stop talking. It had something to do with Seth being next to her.

"I guess I'm just babbling," she said finally.

He grinned at her. "No, it's okay. It's interesting."

Eli saved her from the embarrassment of saying anything else by bringing everybody to a halt. He made them bring their horses up next to his so they could see out across the land.

Lisa had never seen anything like it. In front of them—below them, really—lay a long, thin valley surrounded by snowcapped mountains. "This is Victoria Pass," Eli said. "And that's where we're going." He pointed to the far end of the valley where one mountain, far higher than the others, seemed to stand guard. "The next section of our ride is downhill into the pass and can be quite dangerous. Everybody"—he paused for effect—"and I mean *everybody*, has to follow my lead. You've got to keep your heels down and *don't* lean forward. That helps balance the horse and you. Walk your horses and keep one and a half horse lengths between horses. Are you ready?"

"You bet!" Amy said. The excitement practically bubbled over in her voice.

Eli took that as agreement. "Then let's go!"

He turned his horse onto the narrow trail with a half dozen switchbacks that led down to the floor of the pass. The others followed in turn.

Lisa was behind Stevie and in front of Seth. Amy was the last rider before Jeannie, who brought up the rear.

At first the path was extremely treacherous. It wound

down the hillside, snaking back and forth. The horses needed to be given enough rein so they could pick their own ways along the rocky trail. Although Lisa wouldn't have wanted to admit it, she was glad for the pommel and saddle horn that kept her from slipping over the saddle and onto Chocolate's neck. She held onto it tightly.

"Thank heaven for the saddle horn!" Stevie said over her shoulder.

"Just what I was thinking," Lisa confessed.

Then, as Lisa was wondering if Chocolate could take another step down, the trail made a final hairpin turn and leveled off a little. It still wasn't level by any means, but it was leveler than it had been. It was also still very narrow, edged by bushes clinging to the sharp drop-off.

"Whew!" Lisa said.

"Double that for me," Stevie agreed. "Is everybody down?"

Lisa looked over her shoulder. Seth was right behind her, and Amy was behind him.

"Everybody but Jeannie," Lisa said. "I'm sure she's—"

"Ya-hoooo!" came a loud cry from behind.

Lisa turned around again. She could barely believe her eyes. There was Amy, kicking her horse's belly as if she wanted him to win a race. He responded obediently, breaking into a trot and then a lope. Amy and her horse brushed past Seth and were headed for Lisa, who was at a very narrow part of the trail. There was no way Amy could pass her, and no way she could stop the horse in time.

Lisa did the only thing she could think to do. She gave Chocolate a nudge. The horse didn't need much encouragement. She was as startled by the sounds behind her as Lisa had been. Chocolate broke into a trot, nudging up behind Berry, who had begun walking faster.

Berry was a fast horse and a temperamental one. Lisa didn't want to let either Chocolate or Amy's horse get into a tangle with him. As soon as Amy's horse drew next to Chocolate, Lisa did what she'd seen Jeannie do. She reached out across the gap between her horse and Amy's and grabbed the reins. She tugged sharply. It wasn't the signal Amy's horse was used to, but the meaning was clear. The horse stopped quickly.

"Are you okay, Amy?" Seth asked, drawing up to them.

Stevie turned around then to see what had happened. "Come on, guys," she called back to Lisa, Amy, and Seth. "Let's keep this moving."

"My thoughts exactly," Amy said.

"So you are okay?" Seth asked.

"Of course," Amy said. "I'm always okay."

Lisa began to wonder if that was true.

At that moment Jeannie's horse made it around the final sharp curve of the trail onto the more level area.

"Everything okay up there?" she asked.

"Just fine!" Seth called out cheerfully. "We were just chatting and giving our horses a rest."

"Good idea," Jeannie said. "That was a steep path. They deserve a break. Now I think we'd better catch up with the others. Ready?"

Lisa answered by signaling Chocolate to begin walking again. Her thoughts were focused on Amy and Seth. Poor Seth had to work so hard to make things be all right for Amy! She felt sorry for him and wondered if she could help him at all. She certainly hoped so.

5

"I NEVER THOUGHT I'd say it felt good to be *off* a horse!" Carole said to John.

It was late afternoon, and the group had chosen their campsite for the night. The two of them were carrying grain for the horses to the temporary corral.

"We rode for almost six hours, with just a short break for lunch," John reminded her. "That's enough time in the saddle to test even the most hardened, uh—" He stopped, obviously groping for a polite word. Then he blushed.

"Mine, too," Carole agreed, saving him the trouble. They laughed. "But it really doesn't matter because I loved every minute of it."

"Me, too," he said.

Carole and John had been riding next to each other for much of the day. Carole found she liked him a lot. They had a lot to talk about because he knew almost as much about horses as she did. He had definitely decided to be a veterinarian, and he had already learned a tremendous amount about it. Carole loved listening to his ideas about horse care. It was true that sometimes he could be a little *too* knowledgeable, but after all, that was what her friends said about her!

"Let's give this horse a couple of extra carrots," Carole suggested, patting the gray gelding named Ashley that Amy had been riding all day.

"There aren't enough carrots in the bag to make up for what she did to him coming down that hill," John said.

"You really saw her kick him?" she asked.

"Absolutely," he said. "No doubt about it. I heard her telling Seth that Ashley just ran away with her, but I saw differently with my own eyes."

"Why didn't you say anything?" Carole asked.

John shrugged. "It's none of my business," he told her. "Amy is trouble, and Seth is her brother. He thinks he can handle her. What could I do?"

There didn't seem to be an answer to that. Carole reached into her pocket and fished out a couple of carrot sticks for Ashley. There was a lump of sugar there, too, that she'd brought specially for Berry, but she gave that to Ashley as well. He really had earned it.

KATE AND CHRISTINE were in charge of pitching one of the tents at the campsite. Stevie and Amy were attempting to put up the other one.

"I think this thing attaches to this," Stevie said to Amy. She held a piece of nylon tent in one hand and pointed to a clip on the tent frame with the other.

"I thought it went over there," Amy said.

"Maybe," Stevie said thoughtfully.

Tents were not Stevie's strong point. Somehow she'd always managed to evade this job on sleep-outs. Tonight she obviously wasn't going to be so lucky, but it was clear she had a soul mate in Amy.

"Look," Amy said. "If we just clip everything we see to the nearest grommet, that should do it, right? After all, the instructions probably say the darn thing can be assembled by a six-year-old. If we add our ages together, we'll equal about four six-year-olds."

Stevie giggled. That kind of thinking made sense to her. She began attaching tent to frame as fast as she could. Within about five minutes the whole thing looked more or less like a tent.

"Nice job!" Amy said, congratulating herself.

Stevie agreed. "Not bad work for a bunch of six-year-olds."

"Is that the best you can do on that?" Eli asked. He stood on the far side of the tent with his hands on his hips, regarding their final product.

"Looks pretty good to me," Stevie said, defending their work.

"If it looks right to you, I guess that's what matters most," Eli said. "I'm going to be sleeping in the other tent. This here's the girls' tent, so you can have it just the way you want it."

"We do. Oh, we do," Amy said. "Now, where's the creek where we can soak our feet, and any other sore spots?"

"Right over there," Eli said, pointing to the far side of the campsite. "Just past the place where you're going to help make dinner first."

LISA AND SETH were in charge of finding kindling for the camp fire. It wasn't a difficult task. They were camping in a wooded area, and the ground was littered with dry sticks. They worked side by side without talking much for a while, filling up a bag with the twigs.

Lisa wanted to say something, but Seth seemed preoccupied. There were times, she had learned, when silence was the best conversation. She waited.

"I'm worried about Amy," he said at last. "She's so upset all the time that it's like she has no control over what she does."

"I can tell," Lisa said.

"You can?"

Lisa nodded. "Sure. The things she did today were pretty wild, and the stunt on the downhill path was downright dangerous. Nobody who was thinking straight would do those things. It's like she doesn't care—"

"That's exactly it," Seth said. "She doesn't care. It's because of our parents, see," he began. Then he paused, apparently trying to collect his thoughts.

Lisa wondered what their parents could have to do with Amy's irresponsible behavior.

"They've split up," Seth said.

Lisa remembered that Seth had mentioned that their *mother* had a stableful of horses. He hadn't said anything about their father.

"Dad has his own company in Chicago, and he works all the time. Mom left a year ago and got married again right away. Her new husband is an investor or something, and he runs all of his business out of what he calls his ranch. It's about a million acres."

Lisa had the funny feeling that Seth's statement about the acreage of his stepfather's ranch wasn't much of an exaggeration. She didn't think about that for long, though. Instead she thought about how awful she would feel if her own parents were to get divorced. There would be no family trips, no family meals, no more jokes around the barbecue grill. Holidays would be divided between her parents, and then there might even be new step-parents to cope with. It would be terrible.

She shook her head to ward off the thought, and her heart went out to Seth and Amy, who were actually enduring all the awful things that were racing through her mind.

"Oh, wow," Lisa said. "That must really be tough. I can just imagine how much I would hate it if it happened to me."

"It is tough," Seth said. "And Amy has had a bad time trying to get used to it. She's always been a little wild, but ever since the split it seems like the only person she can count on is me."

Lisa stuffed a few more twigs into the sack. It was almost full. She looked around for a place to sit. A fallen tree provided a bench, and Seth sat down next to her.

"That makes it doubly hard on you, then, doesn't it?" Lisa asked.

"I guess so," Seth said. "I usually just think about how tough it is on Amy, though."

That was so selfless of him, Lisa thought. There he was, with his own worries about his parents, and all he can think about is how hard it is on his sister. Her heart went out to him. Lisa was sure that there must be something she could do to make things easier for Seth. After all, he deserved to have somebody look out for him. And if things went better for Seth, they'd surely be better for Amy.

"How's the twig supply?" Seth asked, changing the subject.

Lisa looked into the bag. "We're about done, but I suppose we could pick up a few more, just in case."

They stood up and walked deeper into the woods.

"We'd better get extra. This stuff will burn up in no time," Seth said, handing Lisa another handful of twigs.

"What do you mean?" Lisa asked.

"It's dry," he said. He took a couple of twigs and crushed them in his hand. "It'll go fast."

It took only a few more minutes to fill the rest of the bag. Then the two of them headed back for the campsite.

The woods were dense on the mountainside, darkly shaded by tall evergreen trees that provided a smooth forest floor and cushioned their footsteps. Lisa listened for familiar forest sounds. Here and there birds called to one another. The fresh breeze whistled through the pine boughs. Then she heard something else. It was a loud, shrill call.

"Listen!" Lisa said excitedly.

"What is it?"

"I think it could be a bobcat," Lisa said.

"A lion!" Seth exclaimed.

"No, a bobcat. It's a kind of lynx. They live in woods like this."

"Are you sure?"

"No," Lisa said. "They do have a sort of screechy cry, but sounds can get distorted from echoes off the mountains. Let's be quiet. Maybe we'll hear it again."

"Let's not wait," Seth said. Lisa was surprised. He was clearly afraid.

"If it is a bobcat, he's no threat to us," Lisa said. "They would never attack humans. Of course, I wouldn't want to get between a bobcat and its supper. . . ." She said it to tease Seth, but it had a stronger effect than she had expected.

"I'm out of here," he said. He dropped the bag of sticks and fled, leaving an astonished Lisa behind.

She picked up the bag and ran after him. "Hey, slow

down!" she called. "There's nothing to worry about—except that you're going the wrong way. Seth! This way!"

Eventually Seth stopped and turned around. Lisa showed him the path and led him straight back to the campsite. They didn't hear the animal cry again, and Lisa was a little disappointed. She was hoping to find out what it was. However, considering Seth's reaction, she figured it was just as well.

"YOU SHOULD HAVE seen her!" Seth said at the camp fire that night. "She wasn't scared at all. There we were, in the middle of nowhere, and there's this incredible screech of a—get this—lion! And he sounds hungry! Does Lisa flinch? She does not! Cool as can be, she takes my arm—she couldn't have held onto my legs, they were shaking so hard—and she keeps me from running right toward the beast. Lisa Atwood is really something!"

As if to emphasize his point, he clapped her on the back. Lisa blushed. It didn't seem to her that she'd really done much for Seth. In spite of what he said, the biggest danger they'd faced in the woods was him running in the wrong direction.

"Of course she's really something," Carole said. "We've always known that."

"Hear, hear," said Stevie.

"My hero!" Amy declared, but Lisa sensed more than a touch of sarcasm in her voice.

"Come on, guys, you're embarrassing me," Lisa said. "It was just a bobcat if it was anything—"

"Speaking of scary things," Amy began. "Isn't it time to talk about something else? Like were you guys listening to the radio in the car yesterday about the escaped monster?"

"You mean the half-human thing that's been in the asylum since it ate all those raw chickens?" Stevie chirped in.

Amy nodded solemnly. Stevie grinned to herself and winked at Amy. This was Stevie's kind of story. In her opinion the very best camp-fire stories always began with some kind of creepy monster loose nearby and known to be attracted to fire. She and Amy obviously agreed on that. It didn't matter that they hadn't even had the radio on in the car yesterday, and it didn't matter that everybody sitting around the camp fire that night knew they were making it all up. Stevie would have bet almost anything that the hairs on the backs of a few necks around the camp fire were standing straight on end. Number one on her list was Amy's brother, Seth.

"And every time they catch it, they put more bars on its cage," Amy continued. "But nothing is strong enough to hold it captive for long. It has this compulsion to stalk its prey by firelight."

Nearby something startled one of the horses, and it whinnied loudly.

"What was that?" Seth blurted out.

Stevie stifled a giggle.

"Oh, probably nothing," Amy said.

"Don't worry, Seth, it's just a story," Lisa told him. He seemed to calm down, but she noticed that later, when Eli suggested that a couple of them check on the horses before they got into their sleeping bags, Seth didn't offer to go.

Lisa understood. Seth had had a very rough time with his parents' divorce. He felt a lot of responsibility for his sister. What he really seemed to need the most was somebody to take care of him. It was a good thing she was there.

6

STEVIE SHIFTED IN her saddle. It was still early morning, and the pack trippers were already on their way, in spite of the fog and the chill morning air. Stevie hadn't slept very well. Neither had anyone else in the girls' tent. The problem was that the tent had lots of openings that let in the chilly breezes. All night long the girls had grumbled about the way the tent had been set up. Amy insisted that it wasn't their fault. It was just that the tent hadn't been properly made. It was *supposed* to have all those air holes in it, to let in breezes on hot nights. Nobody, including Stevie, believed that story any more than they had the one about the monster. Stevie had kept her mouth shut. Nobody would have heard what she said anyway, since she was curled inside her sleeping bag.

Now they were back on the trail. Stevie was still chilled, and she couldn't wait for the morning sun to dry up the fog and bake them warm again.

The trail followed the long rolling valley, rising and dipping with the foothills of the mountains that surrounded the area. There were surprises with every rise. They were crossing an open prairie, which was covered with short grass and crossed here and there with rivulets that fed larger streams. Soon, Stevie could see, they would be entering another forest area and on the other side of that—well, she'd just have to wait and see.

The most astonishing aspect of Victoria Pass, however, was the constant presence of the mountains that surrounded it. To either side the prairie gave way to steep hills, then to thick evergreen forests above, and then, reaching to the sky, craggy mountainsides finally became snowcapped. The mountains were omnipresent, yet so distant that they seemed almost mystical.

"I'm afraid that if I blink, they'll disappear," Stevie said to Christine, who was riding next to her.

Christine smiled. "Sometimes I think that mountains are nature's way of reminding us that the earth has been around a lot longer than we have."

"They do have that effect, definitely," Stevie agreed.

"And the wind, too—the *cold* wind," Christine added. Stevie didn't say anything. "Like the wind that came into our poorly assembled tent last night."

"Really? I didn't notice anything," Stevie said finally. She had the funny feeling that Christine didn't believe her.

CAROLE COULDN'T DECIDE which she liked best: the meadow part of the trail or the wooded part. She loved the vast view from the high mountain meadow, but she also loved the pine smell of the forest. She discussed the issue with John.

"Yes," he said.

"Yes, what?" she asked. "Which do you like best?"

"Yes means I like them both."

Carole laughed. "Yes" was a good answer to the question.

It was getting warmer. Carole removed her windbreaker and her sweater and tied them around her waist. She was glad for the cowboy hat that kept the bright sunshine off her face and neck and out of her eyes. Soon she was rolling up her sleeves and wishing for a cool breeze.

From the front of the line, Eli began singing. He had a

nice voice, which carried back to the other riders. Soon Carole and the others joined in on the familiar cowboy song, "The Streets of Laredo." Carole had never been much of a singer and always found herself embarrassed to sing in public, even in groups, but there was something suggestive about the even beat of the horses' footsteps at the walk that made singing seem like a logical activity. When Eli moved them up to a trot, they changed songs, shifting to the brisker "Camptown Races."

Pretty soon the whole group was singing cheerfully together, and all unpleasant thoughts had flown from their minds. Nobody was thinking about the cold night or about Amy's high jinks on the trail the previous day. They were simply doing what they'd come to do. They were having fun.

"Hey, let's do the one Gene Autrey used to sing," Lisa called out to the other riders.

"'I'm back in the saddle again!'" Eli began, but it turned out that nobody, not even Eli, knew enough words to sing that one, so they tried making up nonsense words to it. Everybody took turns. Not surprisingly, Amy was excellent at nonsense words.

"I sat in the saddle all day.

"Too bad my horse ran away!

"Since my horse was not there,

"I used my saddle for a chair,

"And I guess in this town, I'll just stay!"

There was applause when she finished, and demands for another verse. "Okay, I've got another," she said. Then she began.

"I'm out here, where my dog is my friend.

"I guess we'll be friends to the end.

"We just ride here by the hour

"Where it's hot and we can't shower.

"No wonder there's nobody to befriend!"

Carole and the other riders applauded again. Amy was very clever, and at that moment Carole was glad she was along on the trip.

When the sun was high in the sky, Eli led the riders off the trail, through a small patch of woods, and into a shady open area for a rest and some lunch. First, it was rest time for the horses. Everyone pitched in to untack them and let them drink from a nearby lake surrounded by rocks before they hobbled them in a grassy field near the water.

"Perfect!" Stevie announced when she spotted it. "It was obviously put here to give us a place to swim on this hot, dusty day!"

"No question about it," Kate agreed.

"Definitely," Christine chimed in.

"Can we?" Lisa asked Eli.

"Don't know why not, as long as you're careful," Eli said. "Tell you what. You've been such good singers and riders this morning that Jeannie and I will make the sandwiches while you all take a dip. Then you all can clean up after lunch while we take our swim. Deal?"

"Deal!"

"Do I have to remind you that you should never dive in unfamiliar water, especially since it's been a long, dry summer and the water may be much shallower than you think?"

"We promise, no diving and we'll be super careful," John assured Eli.

"Everybody promise?" Eli asked, looking directly at Amy.

She crossed her heart as she promised.

It took only a few minutes for the riders to don their bathing suits and head for the pond.

"Last one in is a—hey, Amy!" Stevie shouted. Everybody turned to look. Amy had climbed to a rocky ledge five feet above the water and was flexing her knees and swinging her arms.

"No diving!" John called out.

Amy grinned mischievously. She crossed her heart, just as she had when promising Eli she wouldn't dive, and without further ado she jumped high off the rock, tipped forward, touched her toes, straightened out, and dived straight into the water.

"Amy!" Seth shrieked.

Nobody else spoke or moved. They waited. Although the water was clear, the sun sparkled on it, making it difficult to see below the surface. There was no sign of Amy.

Seth ran for the water, ready to jump in after his sister.

John grabbed him. "You can't dive in after her," John reasoned. "Then we'll just have two people to rescue."

Lisa could barely believe the scene that was unfolding before her eyes. She'd been counting silently since Amy's dive. It had been almost a minute, and there was still no sign of her. Now even the bubbles from her dive had dissipated.

Without thinking Lisa dropped her towel and hurried to the edge of the pond. She didn't dive in, but she lowered herself into the cool water quickly and swam over to the place where Amy had disappeared.

Lisa looked around in the water below. She didn't see anything. She also couldn't see how deep it was. She would have to go down there herself.

She took a deep breath and went under. When she opened her eyes under the water, everything was fuzzy.

She could make out a few objects, like the large boulders that cluttered the bottom of the pond. There were stalks of pond grass growing at the floor. There was some movement that might even be fish. There was nothing that looked at all like Amy.

Lisa pulled herself as far down into the water as she could. The water was deep where Amy had dived. Lisa couldn't even reach the bottom on one breath. It didn't make sense that anything would have happened to Amy.

Lisa searched frantically, aware that her lungs were aching for fresh air. She tried to fight the urge to return to the surface, certain that if she could just go a little deeper, swim a little farther, maybe she could find Amy. Maybe she could save her. . . .

Lisa couldn't hold it anymore. She fled to the surface and gasped for breath when she reached it.

"I didn't see anything," she said, panting. "I'll go again!"

She filled her lungs with air and went down again, this time searching to the left and the right, her eyes straining with the discomfort of the water. But there was still no sign of Amy. Once again she returned to the surface.

"Nothing," she said. "There's nothing there at all."

"Oh, no, Amy!" Seth cried out.

"*Moi?*" a voice answered from the cattails. It was followed by a familiar giggle.

"Amy? Is that you? Are you okay?" Seth ran around the edge of the pond in time to see his sister stand up in the middle of the reeds.

"I'm just fine," she announced cheerfully. "I've always liked cattails. Haven't you? I'd like to pick a few, but the stems are so tough. Did you bring your knife?"

Lisa felt a tremendous rush of relief. When she hadn't been able to see anything in the water, she was sure of the worst. Now she could hear the brother and sister chatting in the cattails, and she was so filled with relief that there wasn't room for anything else in her heart.

Stevie, Carole, John, Kate, and Christine stood stunned on the edge of the pond.

"Come on in, the water's fine," Lisa invited them. They stared at her in surprise, expecting her to be at least a little bit angry. Lisa shrugged in answer to the questions in their eyes. "Amy's fine, so am I. No harm done."

"Maybe she's right," Carole said to the others on the shore. "Besides, it's still hot out here and cool in there." One by one they dropped their towels and joined Lisa in the water.

Later Lisa pulled herself out of the water and lay on her towel in the sun to dry off. Kate and Christine joined her.

"Wasn't that wonderful?" Lisa said.

"Part of it," Kate said. "I mean the part where we were all swimming carefully and sensibly. Not the part where someone took a reckless risk, endangering somebody else who tried to rescue her."

"I wasn't in danger," Lisa protested. "It's perfectly safe there. The water is more than ten feet deep."

"True," Christine countered. "But you didn't know that at the time. You could have been swimming down into four feet of water covering dangerous sharp rocks."

"But at least Amy's okay," Lisa said.

"Sure Amy's okay," Kate said. "Amy will always be okay, or else she won't be, and it will be her own fault. It's *Lisa* I'm worried about."

"She's trouble, Lisa," Christine said. "Amy is the kind of person who will always be getting herself, and anybody else she can bring along, into lots and lots of trouble."

"You don't understand," said Lisa. "She's had a hard life. Her parents are divorced—"

"Lots of parents are divorced," Kate said. "That doesn't give their children the right to risk their lives."

"Or anybody else's," Christine finished.

Lisa propped herself up on her elbows and looked at her friends. "Amy isn't the only person in that family," she said. "There's Seth, too. He's got his hands full with Amy, and I really feel sorry for him. I just want to help."

"Helping isn't going to help," Kate said.

Stevie pulled herself out of the water and spread her towel out next to the cluster of her friends. "What's up?" she asked. "Am I missing a Saddle Club meeting?"

"Sort of," Kate told her. "The kind where we help other members, even when they don't know they need help."

"Only in this case they're trying to tell me *not* to help someone else, namely Amy."

"She can be pretty funny," Stevie said, recalling some of her song lyrics.

"Sure. *Sometimes,*" Kate said pointedly.

"If you like sick jokes," Christine added.

"All she needs is a little help," Lisa insisted.

"What she needs is a *lot* of help," Kate replied.

Lisa knew that Kate meant well and that she was probably right about Amy, at least to some degree. But what Kate didn't understand was that Lisa wasn't helping Amy so much as she was helping Seth. Maybe Amy couldn't be helped, but she was convinced that Seth could be. Moreover, she was convinced that she was the one who could do it.

7

"I THINK WE have about two hours before dark," Eli said to the young riders after dinner that night. "Jeannie and I are going to relax here by the camp fire while you all go on a scavenger hunt. Two teams of four." He looked at the group assembled in front of him and put Carole, Kate, Christine, and John on one team. Lisa, Stevie, Seth, and Amy were the second team. "Here are your lists." He handed them to Christine and Seth. "The first team back with everything wins breakfast in bed, delivered by the other team. Everybody is due back here by dark. If neither team gets everything, then the team with the most items wins. Got it?"

They nodded.

"Then, go!"

Carole, Kate, and John circled Christine so they could read the list.

"Bird's nest, piece of granite, animal tooth, pine cone . . ." Carole read.

"I know just where to start," John announced. "Come on, this way."

The team headed to the east, following John. As they left the campsite, Carole could already hear bickering from the other team. Amy was at the center of it. "Let *me* have the list," she whined to Seth. Carole was glad Amy wasn't on her team.

"The hardest thing on this list is going to be the bird's nest," Kate said.

"Oh, no, it's not," John said. "I saw one when Carole and I were watering the horses. It's up in a pine tree not far from here."

John knew right where to go. He took them to a scraggly pine tree that bordered the field where the horses were pastured. "See, it's up there," he said, pointing.

It was up, all right. It was about twenty feet up, and the lowest branches on the tree were a good eight feet above the ground.

"There's a little problem, John," Christine said politely.

"Here, stand on my shoulders," he offered. "One of you should be able to reach from there, don't you think?"

Carole didn't think it would work, but she figured it was worth a try. She was the tallest of the three girls, so she volunteered, but it was clear almost instantly that it just wasn't enough.

"Now if you were a basketball player . . ." she teased.

"I *do* play basketball," John protested.

"NBA," Carole specified.

"It's not the sport, it's the height," Christine said. "We just need somebody taller."

"We've *got* somebody taller!" Kate announced triumphantly. Then, before anybody could ask what she meant, she whistled loudly. The horses, who had been grazing lazily on the other side of the field, pricked up their ears and moved toward the familiar sound. Kate whistled again. Her horse, an Appaloosa named Spot, arrived first.

"I think he's tall enough," she said.

"Great idea!" John agreed. He hiked himself up onto Spot's back and, using his legs to guide the horse, rode him directly under the lowest branch.

Kate and Christine held Spot's halter while John rose to a standing position on the horse's back.

"People in the circus always make this look so easy," he said, using his hands to balance himself.

"In the circus they use draft horses with very wide backs. An Appaloosa doesn't have that same broad, flat surface," Kate said.

"I noticed," he told the girls. "But I am as nimble as an aerialist and can rise above all adversity." With that he grabbed onto the lowest branch and drew himself up into the feathery needles of the tree. Soon he was standing securely, looking for the next branch to climb on.

"Not only can he rise above adversity, he can even rise above the ground!" Christine joked. In response a bird's nest hit her on the head before it tumbled to the ground.

"One down, nine to go," John declared. He jumped down from the branch and landed safely next to Spot.

"Thanks, boy," he said, patting the horse's neck warmly. Spot looked at him expectantly. The look said *carrot*.

"I've tried to teach him not to beg," Kate joked.

"It's okay," John said. "I understand. It's just that I don't have any carrots. All I've got is a bird's nest, and he can't have that."

Spot returned to the herd followed by promises of carrots in the morning.

"Okay, what's next on the list?" John asked.

"A pine cone, and it's right here," Carole said, picking up one from under the tree. And here's a rock. Is it granite?"

Kate, who had taken some geology in sixth grade, examined the rock. She said she thought it looked as if it were probably granite, and by the time they got back to the campsite, it would be too dark to tell anyway.

"Check it off," she announced authoritatively.

It took a little longer to find some of the other items. They combed the bases of four oak trees before locating a single acorn that had been overlooked by all the local squirrels, and they had to comb a whole field before coming across one scraggly crow feather.

"How do we know it's a crow feather?" Christine asked, looking at the weathered sample they had finally located.

"How will Eli know it's *not*?" John countered.

The logic was compelling. They checked the feather off their list, too.

It was easy to find an ant but hard to hold onto it. None of them wanted to kill it. Carole fished in her pocket and found a small plastic bag with a zipper closure. Carole lured the ant into it with some leftover sandwich crumbs and blew the bag up like a balloon before sealing it so the guest would have as much air as possible.

"It still might suffocate before we get it to Eli," John said.

"That's true," Kate said. "But at least we've tried, right?"

"Right," John agreed.

By the time the sun was dipping toward the mountains, they had nine of the ten items on their list. The only thing they hadn't been able to get was an animal tooth.

"I was sure we'd see something," John said. "I've been looking out for a rodent skeleton. They're usually not hard to find, but there hasn't been anything."

Carole had an idea, but it might not be easy. "What kind of animal do you think Eli had in mind?" she asked.

"Any kind of animal," Kate said. "But I think John's right that it's got to be a dead one, because you can't exactly go up to your friendly neighborhood fox and ask him to open wide, can you?" Kate said.

"Fox, no, but an animal's an animal, right?" Carole asked.

"What are you getting at?" John said, sensing that there was an idea lurking behind the questions.

"It's about this tooth," Carole said. She stuck her tongue back to a wobbly bicuspid in her mouth and wiggled. "It'sh prrrry woooofe now," she announced.

"Huh?" John asked.

Kate's face brightened as she understood. "Outstanding!" she said.

John still looked confused. He looked to Kate for a translation.

"She's got a loose tooth," Kate explained. "The only question is *how* loose?"

Carole tested it some more. "I fink it'f abouw rehhy," she said. "Oou wook, okay?"

She opened wide. One by one Kate, Christine, and John checked it out. They agreed that it was about ready. When Carole wiggled it with her tongue, the tooth came completely out on one side.

"Look, you can already see the new one there. It's ready. Definitely."

John's eyes lit up. "Eli's never going to believe this," he said.

"Oh, sure he will," Carole disagreed. "Eli's not going to be the problem. I mean, what am I going to tell the Tooth Fairy?"

Kate, Christine, and John all howled with laughter. When Carole had their promise to pay her the money if her father doubted the story, she sat down on a rock and went to work on her tooth.

First, she wiggled it more with her tongue.

"These big ones are tough," she said. "It was easier with the front teeth."

"You can do it!" Christine said, cheering her on.

Carole switched from her tongue-wiggling technique to the single-digit finger wiggle.

"Ish woohking!" she announced, feeling the tooth loosen even more.

Kate, Christine, and John made a circle around her and continued cheering her on.

"Think of it—breakfast in bed, served by spoiled brat Amy!" Kate said.

That did it. The moment that thought crossed Carole's mind, the tooth was released.

"Ta da!" Carole announced. "One animal tooth for Eli!"

They added Carole's tooth to their collection and hurried back to the campsite.

Eli and Jeannie were waiting for them. There was no sign of the other team.

"We won!" they shouted triumphantly as they handed their booty over to Eli and Jeannie.

Each item had a story, and they loved telling them all to Eli and Jeannie. Eli and Jeannie laughed especially hard when they heard about Carole's tooth.

"I can just see you three bloodthirsty scavenger hunters

standing around poor Carole, trying to get her to yank the tooth out of her head!" Jeannie said.

"It wasn't them that made me do it," Carole confessed. "It was the idea of Amy serving me breakfast tomorrow morning. I'd undergo all kinds of pain just for that!"

"Uh, speaking of Amy," Eli said. "We haven't heard a peep out of that group, and it's getting dark. Did you see them on your hunt?"

Carole shook her head. "The last I saw of them, they were arguing over who was going to hold the list."

"And then they went off to the west," Jeannie said. A worried look crossed her face as she glanced off in the direction the team had taken.

"Take it easy," Carole cautioned. "Seth may be a flake and Amy may be hopeless, but Stevie and Lisa are with them. Those two are levelheaded."

"And creative," Kate said. "If something's gone wrong, they'll know what to do."

"I'M NOT READY to stand up yet!" Amy whined. "Just wait a minute, will you?"

Stevie put her hands on her hips. It seemed to her that they had been waiting a lot of minutes for Amy.

"Just what is wrong with your ankle?" Stevie demanded.

"It's hurt, that's what's wrong with it," Amy retorted.

"Of course it's hurt," Stevie said. "You fell off that branch, where you had no business going in the first place. I told you there wasn't any bird's nest there. But what I want to know is, how hurt is it?"

"It's hurt," was all Amy would say.

Stevie growled, and Amy ignored her.

For the moment Stevie was alone with Amy. As soon as Amy had announced that she was injured, Lisa and Seth had been dispatched to get her some cool water for her ankle. She had given them her sweatshirt to soak in a stream, assuring them that she'd be warm enough without it. Now, however, she was shivering as the cool night settled in.

"Can you lend me your sweater?" Amy asked.

For an instant Stevie considered it. After all, it was becoming almost reflexive to do whatever Amy demanded. Then Stevie realized that it was Amy who had insisted that Lisa take her sweatshirt rather than something sensible like her socks. Stevie wasn't going to freeze just to make up for Amy's mistake.

"No," Stevie said finally.

Amy seemed surprised. Stevie didn't care.

"Here's the water," Seth announced, returning with Lisa. They carried a dripping wet sweatshirt.

Seth tried to follow his sister's orders about her ankle. "Not that way," she said. "Use the arms to tie it around—no, not at my foot—my *ankle*!"

"It must hurt her an awful lot," Lisa said.

Stevie thought that might be true. But she was quite sure that if she ever hurt that much, she'd be nicer to the people who were trying to help her than Amy was being to Seth.

When she stopped to think about it, she was pretty sure that she was always nicer to everybody than Amy was. Amy seemed to have a way of going through life, expecting everybody else to do exactly what she wanted them to do, even when what she did was dangerous. Some people thought that Stevie was a little wild and crazy. It was a characteristic that Stevie usually liked about herself. She wasn't afraid to take risks. At first she'd thought that was true of Amy as well, and Stevie had liked that about her. Stevie could forgive a lot in a person who was as kookie as she was. But with Amy there was something more, and Stevie was beginning to realize how much she didn't like it.

There they were, four of them, out in the wilderness on a mountainside with darkness coming fast. They didn't have any flashlights, and they didn't have any compasses. One of them had a sore ankle, and that one small sore ankle could end up being the cause of some very big problems for all of them.

"Stevie? Lisa!"

It was Eli!

"We're over here!" Stevie called out.

"Oh, thank heavens!" Amy said. "He'll be able to carry me back to the campsite!"

Stevie almost laughed. It was the best feeling she'd had for several hours.

8

STEVIE LEANED FORWARD in her saddle and patted Stewball's neck. He deserved extra thanks for the snootful of dust he was taking from the horse in front of him.

They had started on the trail early that morning, right after Stevie's team had finished serving breakfast to Carole's. It had been made a little more difficult by the fact that Amy's ankle bothered her too much for her to help, so three had to do the work of four, but, Stevie told herself, perhaps that was just as well. If Amy had been involved, she certainly would have found a way to mess it up so that somebody else would have had to work even harder!

Amy's ankle miraculously improved at about the moment she had to climb into her saddle (but not before her horse needed to be saddled up). Seth seemed genuinely relieved by her recovery.

Now they were riding along a trail that followed the rise up the mountain. It was open and grassy, but the grass was very dry so that with every step it seemed the horses kicked up more clouds of dust. Stevie found herself following Eli's lead and tying the kerchief she wore around her neck over her mouth and nose.

"How do you like that dust?" Stevie remarked.

Eli turned in his saddle with a grin on his face as if he'd just been waiting for somebody to ask that particular question. "Ah lak it raw!" he drawled, making three syllables out of the last word.

The riders giggled and adjusted their kerchiefs.

"Akshully, ahm so hungry now, ah cud eat a whole sahd a' beef, too," he added.

"I think that means Eli thinks it's time to stop for lunch," Jeannie translated. "Let's look for a stream to water the horses. Then we can eat."

They rode on for another half hour before they found a trickle of water that would pass for a stream. The riders dismounted and let their horses drink.

It was important not to let them drink too much at first, so Carole, Lisa, and Kate were put in charge of minding the horses at the stream while Stevie and John doled out the oats. Seth and Christine helped Jeannie put out the lunch. Amy's ankle was hurting her, so she couldn't help at all.

"We're just stopping for a few minutes," Eli explained. "We still have a long way to go on this mountain, and we need to be off it by nightfall. It's much too cold up here to spend the night."

"I'll light a fire right away," Christine said, looking for nearby kindling.

"I don't think so," Eli told her. "It's mighty dry around here, and lighting a fire is just asking for trouble. We'll just eat the cold food we've got."

"You think we could start a forest fire or something?" Stevie asked, overhearing his answer. Stevie still had very vivid memories of a barn fire she and her friends had witnessed at riding camp. Although in the end nobody had been hurt, the memory of the danger they'd been in was not pleasant.

"Let me put it this way, Stevie. If we don't start a camp fire, we can't possibly start a forest fire."

The lunch stop was a brief one, really more for the horses than for the riders. They were under way again quickly.

Stevie was totally unprepared for the afternoon ride.

As soon as they left their picnic spot, the trail headed almost straight up the mountain. At first their ride continued through open meadows with occasional forest. Then they entered a deep pine forest.

"Am I crazy, or is it getting a lot cooler?" Stevie asked Christine, who rode next to her along the wide path.

"You're not crazy, I'll tell you that," Christine said, retrieving a windbreaker from her saddlebag. "We're headed up, remember?"

"Like up, up?" Stevie asked.

"Yeah, like up, up," Christine confirmed.

Soon the soft breeze whistling through the pines turned into a brisk wind buffeting the horses and riders on a bare, rocky trail. Stevie looked to her left, down the hill. She could see the pine forest they'd emerged from and realized that they were, in fact, above it. Up, up, as she and Christine had designated it. To her right there were no more trees.

"Hey, we're above the tree line," Stevie observed. "There's nothing but rocks up here!"

"That's why they call them the Rockies," Christine told her. "But you're wrong about there being nothing but rocks."

Stevie thought Christine was mistaken. The terrain

was completely barren. How could anything grow when it was so cold, even in the summer?

Stewball trod gingerly on the rocky path. He seemed a little invigorated by the sudden rush of cool air. He teased the clouds of his own breath when he snorted. Just the sight of that made Stevie put on another sweatshirt.

Then Stevie heard an odd sound beneath Stewball's feet. It was a crunch. She looked down and blinked her eyes in disbelief. Stewball had just walked through a patch of snow—and still the path went up!

Soon, all around them, the ground was covered with a few inches of snow.

"This is what you were talking about, isn't it?" Stevie asked Christine.

Christine nodded. "Beautiful, isn't it? It makes me want to stop and draw a picture of it."

"It makes me want to stop all right, but not to draw a picture. Say, Eli!" she called. He turned to her. "Can we take a ten-minute rest?"

Eli looked at his watch. "If you want," he said. "The horses have been doing a lot of work, and they could probably use a break. Okay, everybody—take ten!"

One look at the sparkle in Stevie's eyes, and Carole knew she had something fun in mind. "What's up?" she asked.

"I think it's time for a friendly snowball fight," Stevie announced. "My team is going to assemble behind that rock over there!" She pointed to a large boulder fifty feet off the path.

Carole was definitely up to the challenge. "And mine is to gather over there!" she declared.

The riders split into the same teams they'd had for the scavenger hunt.

"Winner gets breakfast in bed tomorrow!" Stevie called out, forming her first snowball.

"Oh, that'll be great!" Kate yelled. "This time I want poached eggs!"

The first volley of snowballs flew.

It turned out that Amy's ankle was at least temporarily healed, and she was an ace snowball pitcher. This was her kind of game. She and Stevie were a powerful pair when it came to barraging the others with snow. Lisa and Seth were almost as fast at making snowballs as Stevie and Amy were at throwing them. Carole's team was no match for the bombardment, and by the time Eli announced the end of their "rest," Carole, Kate, Christine, and John were ready to admit defeat.

Still giggling, they swept snow off themselves and returned to their horses.

"I hadn't thought of poached eggs," Stevie said to Kate

as she tightened Stewball's cinch. "That sounds like a wonderful idea. I like them with the white mostly firm and the yolk very soft, okay? And freshly squeezed orange juice—"

"You like it cold?" Kate asked, poised to remount Spot.

"Of course," Stevie said.

"Then start with this," she suggested, and tossed one final snowball at Stevie. "Bull's-eye!" she announced when it hit Stevie in the center of her back.

"I guess I probably deserved that, but you still lost the snowball fight, remember that."

Kate grinned at Stevie. "Of course I remember. We lost fair and square. I just wanted to have the chance to get you with a good one."

Stevie put her left boot in the stirrup and swung herself up into Stewball's saddle. "I know what you mean," she said. "There's something about having the last word, even when you've lost the argument."

"Something like that," Kate agreed.

Then Eli and Jeannie gave the signal, and they were on their way. The snow on the ground muffled sounds and made the whole world seem quieter. It almost made it harder to talk. Stevie listened to the hushed clip-clop of horse hooves in the snow and the comfortably familiar squeaking of the leather saddles. Although she was surrounded by friends, she felt their isolation on the mountain. They were so small, so few. It was so grand, so imposing, this fabrication of nature that was too wild to have trees grow on it and so cold that it made snow in the summer. The idea made her feel strangely insignificant.

There weren't many things that could make Stevie feel insignificant. In that way she *was* rather like Amy. The thought of Amy jolted her. She found that she didn't like the idea that she had anything in common with Amy. Thinking about Amy made her think about Lisa. Stevie had barely talked to Lisa since they'd started the ride. Lisa seemed totally involved with Seth, and as far as Stevie could see, Seth was almost as mixed up as his sister. Stevie didn't like the idea of Lisa being drawn into their problems. Lisa was older than she was, but in some ways she seemed younger. When it came to friends, other than her Saddle Club friends, Lisa could be impressionable. She'd get an idea in her head about how wonderful somebody was, and then no matter how wonderful that person *wasn't*, it took Lisa a long time to stop being nice. A lot of the problem was that Lisa was such a nice person herself. Some of it, in this case, was that Lisa just didn't see that Amy was using Seth and Seth was using Lisa.

Then it dawned on Stevie that Lisa could be in trouble. As long as she was part of Amy's schemes, even through Seth, it was dangerous because Amy was dangerous. Stevie wanted to help Lisa, but Stevie knew from experience that just telling her to stay away from Seth and Amy wasn't going to do it. This, Stevie realized, was going to have to be a Saddle Club project. It was a good thing so many people on the trip were in the Saddle Club. With Carole's help, plus Kate's and Christine's, she'd do whatever she had to do to make Lisa see that Amy and Seth were bad news.

Stevie sighed with relief, her breath a little puff of steam in front of her. Now all she had to do was find a way to talk to Carole alone.

9

CAROLE STOWED BERRY'S saddle for the night and looked around the campsite for her next chore. Everywhere people were working busily. The day's ride had been wonderful but long, going all the way up, and then back down, the mountain. All the riders were ready for an early supper and a good night's sleep.

"Give me a hand, will you, Carole?" Stevie asked.

"Sure," Carole responded wearily before she even knew what Stevie wanted her to do. "I'm never too tired to help a friend, except maybe now, but you're a *good* friend. How can I help?"

"I think Stewball picked up a stone. I want to check his hooves."

Carole willingly followed Stevie out of the campsite to the temporary corral but realized quickly that something odd was going on. Stevie was the best stone picker at Pine Hollow. There was no way she needed help.

"What's up?" Carole asked. "I mean, I know you don't need me to help you with a stone in your horse's shoe. That's the lamest excuse—pardon the pun—you ever came up with. Is this some kind of joke? Because if it is, I'm going to remind you how long I've been riding and how tired I am."

"No joke. It's about Lisa," Stevie began, shaking her head with concern. "I think we've got a Saddle Club project on our hands, and I needed to talk to you alone."

"Lisa? What's the matter?" When it came to friends, there was no such thing as being too tired. Carole was wide awake.

"It's not so much Lisa as it is Seth and Amy, really. They've drawn Lisa into their problems, and Lisa just doesn't see how they use each other. Now they're using Lisa, too."

"I noticed," Carole agreed. "Everytime Seth runs to help Amy, Lisa runs to help Seth—even when nobody really needs help."

"Correction," Stevie said. "Both of them need help, but not the kind Lisa can give them."

"I don't know what to do," Carole said.

"Me neither, but we've got to do something."

When they arrived at the corral, they stood and looked at the horses. Somehow they always seemed to be inspirational, just like The Saddle Club.

"I could look at horses for hours," Stevie remarked.

"I could, too," Carole agreed, gazing across the field. "They are so—" Carole stopped and stared at the small herd. Her eyes caught something, and she wasn't sure what it was.

"What's the matter?" Stevie asked, suddenly alarmed.

"I don't know," Carole said. "But look at the horses; something's wrong."

Stevie turned and looked, too. There were all the horses, now gathered in a small area of the field, as if for the protection of the group. All of them looked very alert, ears turning this way and that, tails swishing. A few pawed the ground. Noses were in the air, and nostrils were flared.

"Oh, look!" Carole said, suddenly seeing what was wrong and pointing. There, in a wooded section of a hill across the field and perhaps two miles away, a dark stream of smoke rose steadily.

"A forest fire!" Stevie cried. As both of them stared, the smoke began to billow and turned a deep orange red. Then, suddenly, flames shot up from the sooty mass.

The breeze that had brought the flames to the hillside then brought them the strong, acrid smell of the smoke.

"We've got to get out of here!" Carole said urgently. "Let's get Eli."

She didn't have to say it twice.

"THERE'S A FOREST fire, and it's coming this way!" Carole cried out to Amy, who was sitting on a rock near the temporary corral. She seemed to be putting some kind of support bandage on her ankle, and she barely acknowledged Carole's news.

"I hope we have enough marshmallows," she said.

Since there was no point in wasting time arguing with Amy, Carole and Stevie ran past her to the campsite. By the time they reached it, the smell of smoke had penetrated the woods. Eli hurried back with them to see the view over the corral.

They found that the horses were now very restless, shuffling toward them, away from the approaching fire. The fire, though still small, was growing, fanned by the breeze.

"Look, that's where it came from," Eli said, pointing to a mountainside several miles farther away from them, now clearly burning. "See, some kind of spark or ball of fire rises up out of a larger flame section and leaps ahead of the main body of the fire. That's one way secondary fires start."

"You mean this is just a secondary fire?" Stevie asked.

"*Just* is the wrong word," Eli cautioned her. "It's definitely an offshoot from the other fire, and that makes it secondary. It's still serious, though, and it's still headed this way. Your first instinct was right. We've got to get out of here. If we can get back to the valley, we should be safe, but it's a long trip yet, and it's getting dark. We don't have a second to waste."

Eli told Carole and Stevie to round up the horses and prepare them to be saddled up. He went back to oversee breaking camp. Tired as they and the horses were, there would be no stopping until they were safe.

Carole decided that Stevie should walk into the corral and circle behind the horses, getting them to walk over to where Carole waited with halters and lead ropes. Stevie took a halter with her and slipped it over the head of the farthest horse, who happened to be Stewball. Stevie was glad about that. Whatever else could be said about Stewball, he was smart. Stevie clipped the lead rope on him and began to use him to move the small herd toward Carole.

Some of the horses were balky. Stevie didn't know exactly what to do, as she tried to be in three or four places at once. Carole couldn't help her. She had to stay where she was. Then Amy arrived, obviously sent by Eli and just as obviously reluctant.

"Go help Stevie," Carole said. "She's got to round the herd up and get them over here."

"Oh, go boss someone else," Amy said. "Your know-it-all act doesn't work with me."

Stevie couldn't hear what was being said, but she could see that Carole was having trouble with Amy. The air was growing dim from the approaching smoke. They didn't have time for trouble. They didn't have time for Amy.

While some of the horses in the herd moved slowly and nervously toward Carole, others pranced and galloped every which way. Kate's Appaloosa shot past Stevie and Stewball, running to the far side of the paddock. Another horse took two steps to the left and stood frozen, completely panicked. Stevie was near panic herself.

Just then help arrived, in the form of a four-legged expert at herding. Eli's dog, Mel, came bounding across the field to Stevie.

"Eli always said you were the smartest creature he

knew," Stevie said. "Now you have a chance to show me just how right he is."

The first thing Mel did was to run around the field, as if she needed to figure out the lay of the land. Then, once she knew what had to be done, she got to work. She stood flat-footed by the horse who was frozen in fear and barked. It took only a few seconds for the horse to decide that he was more afraid of Mel than he was of the fire. He turned on his heels and trotted willingly to Carole, who put on his halter and lead rope.

Mel's next target was the Appaloosa, who had run toward the fire. The dog circled on the far side of the horse, wagged her tail briskly, and changed the horse's mind. Spot trotted over to Carole.

Stevie was so fascinated by Mel's herding technique that she almost forgot how important it was to finish the job quickly. However, with Mel's help the rest of the horses remained in a herd, and Stevie was able to move them over to where Carole, and by then John, were waiting for them.

When the last horse had a halter and lead rope and had been secured, they began saddling up. Stevie didn't think she'd ever tacked up so many horses so fast in her life. She was working so quickly, she almost didn't notice

Amy, still leaning against a tree. The sight, however, was too much to ignore.

"Get to work, Amy," Stevie said. "The saddles are over there; you can see what needs to be done."

"You're getting pretty bossy, Stevie," Amy retorted. "Sounds to me like you've been spending too much time around the queen boss, Miss Carole Hanson."

Stevie was shocked by Amy's response. Any admiration she had ever had for Amy's boldness fled. So did any sympathy she'd harbored for the girl's family situation. All she felt was fury, flamed by her own fear of the approaching fire. "How dare you?" Stevie exclaimed. "This is no time for your stupid games. As far as I'm concerned, you can take whatever risk you want with your own safety, and you can drag your dumb brother down with you if you want, but when it comes to my safety and the safety of my friends and these wonderful horses, you have no right to act the way you do. Grow up or get out!"

Amy drew herself to her feet and limped away. Stevie didn't consider her departure much of a loss. Amy hadn't shown much talent at tacking up horses anyway.

With Carole, Stevie, and John working as a team, the horses were soon ready. Carole secured the riding horses and stayed with them. John and Stevie took the packhorses along the path to the campsite to facilitate packing. They found Amy once again sitting on a rock near the campsite, fussing with the bandage on her ankle. Stevie was so angry, she didn't even say a word. John didn't, either.

"Where's Amy?" Seth asked as they entered the campsite. "Wasn't she with you?"

Stevie shrugged her shoulders. John told Seth where Amy was.

"Oh," Seth said. "It must be her ankle. She needs help!"

He dropped the tent he had been folding and ran past the packhorses to his sister. Lisa was close on his heels.

John and Stevie secured the packhorses and took up the tent folding where Seth and Lisa had dropped it. Stevie had learned a lot about tents since her first unsuccessful attempt at putting one up, and one thing she'd learned was that there was a lot of material, and it was difficult to fold, especially with only two people. It would have been much easier with more, but with Seth and Lisa hovering over Amy, there was nobody extra to help.

John was methodical and organized, and he and Stevie managed without help. They stowed the tent on the horse and helped Eli, Jeannie, and the other riders put everything else away. At the same time the riders had to pack up their personal belongings to be carried by their own horses. Stevie put Carole's things away, knowing Carole was too busy with the rest of the horses. She packed up Lisa's things, too, because Lisa, after all, was one of her best friends. Kate and Christine helped her. Nobody touched Amy's clothes or belongings.

All the while they were working at top speed, the wind kept bringing reminders of what they were working against. Each gust carried a stronger smell of smoke. Then small animals started overrunning the campsite. When the first squirrel zipped across Stevie's feet, she jumped with surprise. She soon found, however, that it was followed by many more, plus rabbits and a lot of other small animals, including some she didn't even recognize.

"If they're running, we should be, too," Eli said. "I don't want to scare you guys unnecessarily, but I think we should be scared. Anything that's not on a horse's back now, stays. We are out of here."

Eli began jogging, leading one of the packhorses. The others followed, bringing the rest of the horses with them.

"Seth, Amy, Lisa!" Eli called. "Get to your horses. We have to get away from here! *Now!*" He added the last word when he saw how slowly Amy was standing up.

It pained Stevie to see Lisa and Seth each holding one

of Amy's arms across their shoulders. She was sure, beyond any doubt, that Amy was more than capable of walking, even jogging, over to the temporary corral. She was just slowing everybody down with her phony ankle act. Stevie knew enough about fires to know that sometimes seconds counted—and Amy was costing them a lot more than seconds.

"My clothes!" Lisa cried out.

"We got them for you!" Kate assured her. "Get to your horse!"

"Hurry!" Jeannie cried out. "There's no time to waste!"

Stevie had a sickening feeling in her stomach when Jeannie said those words. She knew what Amy's reaction would be. To confirm her suspicions she turned to look just in time to see Amy stumble. Seth and Lisa held her firmly, but it made them lag even farther behind.

"Slow down!" Lisa called. "Wait for us!"

"Meet us at the corral," Christine said. "Your horses are all tacked up there."

Stevie couldn't believe the changes she saw when she reached the corral and the saddled horses. The fire, which had been small and distant the last time she'd seen it, had grown to enormous proportions in less than half an hour. It was now visibly raging on the hillside no more than a mile away. The field that served as their temporary corral buzzed with activity as the small animals continued their flight from the impending fire.

"If these guys are out of here, so am I!" declared Stevie. She mounted Stewball, took the lead rope of one of the packhorses, and began the trail ride of a lifetime.

10

"HURRY, LISA!" CAROLE called to her friend. Lisa was still supporting Amy, who now seemed to be favoring the wrong ankle. Carole had mounted Berry and, like Stevie, held the lead rope of one of the packhorses. Lisa, Seth, and Amy hadn't even reached the corral yet.

"I don't want to leave Seth—he needs my help with Amy!" Lisa protested.

Carole was about to give Lisa a list of twenty reasons why she had to leave Amy and Seth, when the fire did her convincing for her. A flaming ball flew over their heads and into the forest, less than fifteen feet from where Amy was standing. As soon as it landed, the ground cover began smoldering.

Amy screamed. Lisa dropped her arm of support from around the limping girl and ran to her horse. Even Amy started moving a little faster.

"Head along the edge of the meadow there," Eli directed them. The open area skirted the mountain, leading toward the valley. They could move quickly through it, and it would take them away from the fire.

Stevie paused in the meadow and turned back to make sure everybody was safe. She also wanted to wait for Lisa. Jeannie had gone on ahead, followed by Carole, Kate, Christine, and John. Eli had told the riders to drop the lead lines of all the packhorses. Mel would take care of seeing that they followed. Since all the horses appeared very interested in getting away from the fire as quickly as possible now, it seemed that Mel would have a fairly easy job of it. She barked furiously and officiously. The horses meekly obeyed her.

Eli took charge of Seth, who was too frightened by the fire to do anything at all. He even needed help getting into his saddle. When Eli gave Seth's pinto a smack on the rump, the horse loped off to follow the others through the field. Seth clutched the horn of his saddle like a toddler on a merry-go-round.

Lisa loped up to Stevie.

"What's Amy's problem now?" Stevie asked.

"It's her ankle," Lisa explained. "It hurts so much, she can't kick her horse and make it lope."

"That's it," Stevie said. "I'm tired of standing by on this one. It's time for action. Come on!"

With that Stevie turned Stewball around and loped back to where Amy was holding her horse to a walk. The irony of the fact that Amy thought it was okay to lope along a rocky, hilly trail but insisted on a ladylike walk in a fiery field did not escape Stevie. Nor, it appeared, did it escape Lisa.

"Amy, we've had enough of this," Lisa said. "It's time to hurry."

"My ankle—" Amy began.

"My—" Stevie began.

"Ahem," Lisa cut her off, suspecting what she was going to say. "Let's just do the job."

Stevie and Lisa knew exactly what had to be done. They got on either side of Amy. Each reached over and took one of her reins.

"Hold on," Stevie suggested. The two girls urged their horses to a lope. Amy's horse followed very willingly. In fact, the horse was so glad to be moving that he quickly picked up to a gallop, trying to catch up with the rest of the group. As he passed between Chocolate and Stewball, Lisa and Stevie handed the reins back to Amy, who, not surprisingly, had had no trouble at all staying on.

"Miraculous recovery!" Stevie observed wryly.

When Lisa laughed, Stevie sighed with relief. If Lisa could find it funny, it meant the beginning of the end of Amy's hold on her.

Stevie noticed a sudden change in Stewball's gait. He became friskier, prancing to the side. His nostrils flared, and his ears perked up, turning every which way. Stevie looked around, trying to figure out what had changed to make Stewball so tense. The answer came in sight, and it had four feet. A bobcat raced across the field, cutting directly in front of Stewball and Chocolate. As soon as it was gone, Stewball relaxed and resumed his determined lope toward the valley and safety.

"I don't think Stewball had much to fear from that little cat," Stevie said.

"A predator's a predator," Lisa reasoned. "And if that predator is running away from something at that speed, you know it must be frightful."

The two girls looked over to their left, where the fire was growing steadily, just in time to see a tall pine, consumed by flames, tumble onto the far side of the meadow. It ignited the dry prairie grass, and the flames began spreading wildly across the entire meadow.

"Let's get out of here!" Stevie yowled, kicking Stewball's belly. It wasn't a signal she had to give twice. Stewball had eyes and ears, and a nose to smell the smoke. He fled. Chocolate followed suit. Proper riding form dictated that the riders grip with their legs and hold their reins steady, above the level of the saddles, but proper riding form went out the window with the wild gallop that Stewball and Chocolate used to escape the fire. Both girls gripped as tightly as they could with their legs, but they also held onto reins, saddle horn, and mane with all their might. They certainly couldn't afford a fall at the moment.

The field sloped down to the right. Stevie and Lisa caught up with the rest of the riders, just in time to see them reach the edge of the grassy area, where they were forced to return to the woods.

"Follow me!" Eli cried. He waved his arms to signal the beginning of the trail to Stevie and Lisa. Mel circled around the packhorses and brought them into line.

Everything slowed down when they entered the woods. For one thing, it was beginning to get dark, and that made it harder to find and follow the trail. For another thing, smoke from the approaching fire dimmed everything further. The horses went from a gallop to a walk, and events seemed to shift into slow motion—everything, that was, except the approaching fire.

All of Stevie's senses were heightened. With every leaf that crackled under a horse's hoof, she listened for fire. With every breath she took, she feared the smoke was thicker. She could taste it in her mouth, and when she blinked her eyes, now tearing from the discomfort of the acrid smoke, she was afraid she'd miss seeing some danger sign. She longed to feel the cool night air on the bare skin of her arms but felt only the enveloping warmth of approaching flames and the sweat of her own fear. Even a half mile or more away, the fire tingled every one of Stevie's senses.

Carole and Jeannie were at the head of the line of riders and horses. The combination of night and smoke made it almost impossible to see where they were going. Yet the press of danger from the rear urged them on.

"Ease up on your reins," Jeannie advised Carole. "Berry's a smart horse with good instincts," she went on. "He may have a better idea of a safe path than you do."

Jeannie's words made sense to Carole. She relaxed her hold. Berry shook his head for a second, as if to assure himself that he was now in charge. Then he lowered his head and began walking more quickly.

The woods were dark and thick and cloaked in the pitch black of night. Carole really didn't know what direction she was going in. All she was fairly certain of was that she was going away from the fire. That was enough.

From time to time Carole could hear Mel barking. Apparently it was a language Berry understood, because the barking made him adjust his direction, and it always seemed to be for the better. It was so dark in the forest that Carole could feel Berry lowering his head to walk downhill before she could see where he was going. Step by step he made his way down, and then the ground was level. There was the vague sound of trickling water. Carole squinted. Then she understood.

"It's a creek bed—it's almost dry, but I think it's a clear path!" she cried out to the riders behind her. She didn't even stop to wonder how it was that Berry and/or Mel had found the stream. For now it was good news, and that was enough. She leaned forward and gave Berry a very grateful pat on his neck.

"Carrots'll come later," she assured him. "And sugar, and apples, and anything else your little tastebuds desire. Okay?"

Berry didn't answer. He just kept going forward, now at a relaxed trot. Carole felt she had a lot of things to be grateful for right then, not the least of which was the fact that horses could see in the dark.

AS SOON AS her horse was in the creek bed, Lisa paused to let Stevie catch up to her and to let Chocolate have a little drink. In a minute they would be moving faster, but for now she had to take a few seconds to get something off her chest.

"Thank you," she said to her friend.

"For packing up your stuff? It was nothing," Stevie assured her.

"Thank you for that, too, but what I meant was thank you for sticking with me while I was being a jerk about Amy."

"And Seth," Stevie said. "You were an even bigger jerk about him."

"I know. I was hoping you hadn't noticed. He and Amy are hopeless cases, and one day she's going to do something really selfish and dangerous, and she won't be as lucky as she has been."

"I'm not sure I care," Stevie said. "Do you?"

"It nearly took getting killed by a forest fire, but I've figured out that there are times when you can't protect people, even from themselves."

"Welcome back," Stevie said.

"It's nice to be back," Lisa told her. "Now to see that I

stay back, let's get going and catch up with the others. I don't think we're out of this yet."

Her point was emphasized by the thundering crash of a tree less than a hundred yards behind them.

The horses bolted into action, moving as quickly as they could along the stony creek bed.

"WHAT IS IT?" Kate asked Carole. There was some kind of barrier ahead of them in the creek bed.

"I don't know," Carole answered, drawing Berry to a halt. "Mel?" she called out, hoping that once again the brave dog could show her the way.

Mel came instantly, appearing from the darkness. Her tail waved eagerly, and she sniffed her way toward the barrier. Carole waited for the diagnosis. Mel barked.

Berry stepped forward tentatively, and Carole squinted in the darkness. Then Carole could see that a large tree had fallen across the creek bed. It wasn't a result of the fire, since it obviously had been there for some time. The water flowed under it easily, but the horses would have to go around it.

"Find a way, Mel!" Carole urged the dog. Mel stood her ground and barked.

Carole thought maybe Mel didn't understand her, and she didn't know how to make the order clearer. She also thought that since she was at the front of the line of riders, maybe this time it was her job, not Mel's, to forge the path. She dismounted and began to explore.

The tree was enormously long. It had been rooted in a hillside to the right that was much too steep to climb, so there was no path on that side of the creek. On the other side the tree lay tangled in a dense undergrowth that would take hours to cut through. They didn't have hours. They might not even have minutes. Carole returned to the creek bed, checked the ground on either side of the tree trunk, and made her decision.

"Over," was all she said.

She remounted Berry and rode him back in the creek bed about ten yards. She didn't have any idea whether Berry knew how to jump, and she could give him only one chance to learn. Jumping was a skill that English riders worked on for style and precision. Carole was a good rider; she could do this. She hoped.

She took a deep breath and nudged Berry into a canter. She directed him right toward the treek trunk. It was about three feet high and at least as wide. Carefully she took stock of the distance and height. At exactly the right moment, Carole leaned forward and rose out of the saddle, moving her hands forward to give Berry the rein he'd need. Carole felt the surge of power as Berry's strong rear legs propelled him into the air and over the log. He landed smoothly while Carole shifted her weight back into the seat of the saddle.

"No faults!" Kate cried joyously from the far side of the log. Carole laughed, feeling giddy with her success. Competitive jumpers were charged with faults when they made mistakes going over jumps. This wasn't exactly a competition, though. This was real life!

One by one the other riders did just what Carole had done. John's horse refused to jump at first, but he made it over on the second try. A few of the packhorses chose to climb over the log rather than to jump it. It was slower and more cumbersome, but it worked. Seth was too frightened to jump. He dismounted, clambered over the log himself, and then let his horse jump without him. He remounted and was on his way. Not surprisingly, Amy made the jump without difficulty. Stevie and Lisa brought up the rear of the young riders, and Eli came last of all.

On the other side of the log, the creek bed began a gentle slope downward. It became both wider and smoother. The horses automatically began going faster. Stevie sniffed the air. There was a noticeable change for the better.

"There's less smoke," she told Eli. He sniffed and agreed.

"We've come all the way around the mountain, and we're entering the valley now. There's not so much wind here, so the fire should stay on the other side of the mountain. We're not totally out of harm's way yet, but we're not far from safety."

Suddenly a breeze hit Stevie's face. She immediately noticed two things about the breeze. The first was that it was coming toward her face, not at her back. That meant that it also had to be pushing the fire back. The second was that it was fresh, containing no smoke. That meant there was no fire in front of them. And then a third thing came to her about the breeze—it had splattered her face with water.

"Rain!" she cried.

"A lot of it!" Lisa echoed, shielding her eyes from the brisk storm that seemed to have come very suddenly from nowhere.

"Are we safe now?" Lisa asked Eli.

"I think so," he said. "I've been hoping for rain. Now that we've got it, I hope we get enough."

"Yippeee!" Carole and Kate shouted almost in unison. "Doesn't it feel wonderful?"

"Absolutely mahvellous!" Christine confirmed.

"Does somebody have a poncho I can borrow?" Amy asked.

"No," five people answered in chorus.

It took another hour, riding slowly in what turned out to be a drenching rain, for the riders to reach an area close to a lake in the valley where Eli felt they could be assured of safety through the night. It wasn't an easy ride, but the Saddle Club girls and John hardly noticed the difficulty at all. They were too relieved and too tired. The only thing that really seemed to matter was that they were alive, and safe.

11

STEVIE OPENED ONE eye and then closed it again. It couldn't possibly be morning already, could it? The brilliant sunshine peeking through the tent suggested that it was.

Then the whole night came back to her. She remembered the frantic ride through the pitch black, smoke-infested forest, the dramatic jump over the log, the arrival of the soothing, cooling rain, and the fresh breezes that combined with the rain to protect the riders from the onslaught of the forest fire. She remembered their arrival at the campsite, the rush to unsaddle the horses, water them, and secure them for the night in the drenching rain. She recalled helping to pitch the tents hastily and deciding to share a sleeping bag with Carole because they were both too tired to try to find another in the confused mess of camping gear that they were able to unload from the packhorses. After that she didn't recall anything. It had been well past midnight before the riders were ready to sleep. Sleep, when it was finally allowed, came quickly.

Stevie opened both eyes. She hauled her arm out of the sleeping bag and looked at her watch. It was already nine-thirty. She crept out of the sleeping bag, being careful not to disturb Carole, and emerged from the tent into a bright, warm, and sunny day.

"Good morning!" Eli greeted her cheerfully.

"Is everything okay?" she asked, barely able to believe it.

"Just about," he said. "One of the packhorses lost his pack somewhere along the way. We don't have as much food as we would like, but we're really fine, especially if we can catch a few fish from the lakes today. Also, it seems that a lot of personal belongings were abandoned at the campsite in the rush last evening, so some people—"

"Oh, there you are, Stevie," Amy interrupted. "I'm glad you're up, because now you can lend me a clean pair of jeans."

Stevie recalled then that they had left Amy's belongings at the campsite while Amy fiddled with her bandage and refused to help break camp. Although she had several perfectly good pairs of jeans, she couldn't think of a single reason to share them with Amy.

"Sorry, this is all I've got," she lied, and she didn't feel bad about it at all.

Amy stared as if studying Stevie's face for a hint of a lie. Stevie gave her nothing.

"Too bad," Amy said, and went off in search of another victim.

Eli said nothing. He just showed Stevie where she could wash up and accepted her offer to dig for worms for fishing.

Before too long Stevie had a hook baited and had found a comfortable place to sit and pass the time until she could catch some breakfast. Carole and Lisa soon joined her. They were too groggy to talk, but that didn't seem to interfere with their fishing skills. By the time Eli had the camp fire going, they'd caught enough fish among them to make a delicious breakfast for everyone.

"The fish probably smelled the smoke last night. It must have psyched them for a camp fire!" Stevie announced, displaying their catch.

The rest of the riders were up by then, and since there

hadn't been any dinner the night before, breakfast seemed like an awfully good idea.

Jeannie asked Kate and Amy to help her clean the fish. Kate rolled up her sleeves and opened up her pocketknife. Amy just looked at the fish distastefully. Kate had the feeling she was searching for an excuse.

"Is your ankle bothering you?" she asked.

"Quite a bit," Amy said.

"Well, then this is a perfect job because you can do it sitting down," Jeannie said, handing her a sharp knife.

"I think I did quite enough last night," she said. "I don't see why I should have to do any more work today. Seth! Come give me a hand, will you?"

Seth came running. With his help Amy limped off.

"Good riddance," Jeannie declared, picking up the first fish for cleaning.

Stevie decided later that the best part about Amy's limp was that, even with Seth's help, she and Seth were the last ones to arrive when breakfast was served. There were just small morsels of the fresh fish remaining for them. That was enough to put both Seth and Amy into a pout, but it didn't upset anybody else at all.

"Okay," Eli announced after breakfast. "We've got a few things to do. I saw to the horses this morning, but I want each rider to check his or her own mount and do some grooming. Then it's our own turn for some well-deserved grooming. All I will say about that is, the last one into the lake is a rotten egg!"

Stevie, Carole, and Lisa hurried over to the temporary corral together. Kate was already there, along with Christine and John. When Kate whistled, Spot came over to her. The other horses moseyed over as well.

"I think they're as tired as we are," Lisa observed, reaching for Chocolate to give her a hug.

Stevie entered the corral and clipped a lead rope on Stewball. She picked up some grooming gear, and when she'd tied the rope to the branch of a tree, she began working.

"Has Stewball got a bunch of burrs and stuff on him? Chocolate does," Lisa said from the other side of the tree.

"I don't know yet because I just started, but I do know that he's got so many smudges, he almost looks like a chestnut instead of a skewbald. How could anybody get that dirty?"

Lisa stood up and stared at Stevie. Then she started to laugh.

"What's so funny?" Stevie asked.

"You," Lisa said. "But I guess you can't help it. You

don't know it because nobody has a mirror, but you've got even more smudges on you than Stewball does."

"Me?" Stevie asked.

Lisa nodded. Nearby, Carole and Christine nodded, too.

"Okay, okay, so I'll groom myself right after I groom Stewball. The bad news is that I only have enough soap and shampoo for one horse and one person. Poor Amy won't be able to borrow a single bubble from me!"

"Awwww, too bad!" the girls agreed.

IT TURNED OUT that Amy and Seth couldn't even borrow bathing suits, so while everybody else was splashing around in the cool water, the two of them just rinsed their hands and faces and retreated to the campsite, where they sat glumly, complaining about how miserable they were.

Stevie pulled herself out of the water, poured a dab of shampoo in her hand, and lathered up her hair and the rest of herself. She doused herself with a couple of buckets of water to get the suds out and then she dived into the lake and swam as far as she could under water. She splashed up to the surface.

"Oh, that feels wonderful!" she declared.

Once all the swimmers were clean, they began the serious business of play. Eli brought out a Frisbee he'd managed to fit into his pack, and they made a large circle in the water.

"I was going to have us try this on horseback," Eli said. "So to make it an extra challenge, let's try it in the water—over our heads."

That, naturally, led to races for the Frisbee, more than a few dunkings, and finally to an all-out splash battle. When everybody was clean, soaking wet, and nicely exhausted, they pulled themselves out of the lake, spread out their towels, and lay down in the warm sunshine.

The last one out of the lake was Mel. She stood near everybody's towels and shook herself dry. Then she barked.

"What's up, girl?" Eli asked. Mel barked some more in answer.

Everybody sat up and looked around. They'd learned the night before, if they hadn't known it already, that Mel knew when something was going on. If there was danger around, she'd know it first, so they couldn't afford to ignore her.

Stevie sniffed the air. There was no smell of smoke.

Carole scanned the countryside. She didn't see any

smoke or flames, nor were there any dangerous animals in sight.

And then they all heard the sound of an airplane. Soon a small plane appeared through a pass in the mountains that surrounded the valley, flying low, as if it were searching for something.

"It's looking for us!" Jeannie declared.

"Oh, of course," Eli said, realizing what was going on. "My friends with the ranch, where we started out, must have called the authorities to tell them what our plans were. They want to be sure we weren't caught in the fire. Too bad we don't have a radio, or we could let them know we're okay."

"Who needs a radio when we've got a whole lake?" Stevie asked.

Stevie was in action before anybody had a chance to ask what she was doing. There were times, Lisa knew, when you just did what Stevie asked and didn't make trouble. It always seemed to work out. This, she suspected, was one of those times, so when Stevie shooed everybody back into the water, everybody obeyed willingly.

"Two teams of four!" she declared. "You four, make a circle. Hold hands." Carole, Christine, John, and Jeannie did as they were told. "Now, this part is a little trickier. Eli, you and I are the upright of the K. Kate and Lisa, you each have to be the lines that go from the center. . . ."

That was when Lisa figured it out. They were spelling OK for the pilot of the plane, and they were doing it in the water because the bottom of the lake was dark, and the shape of the letters would stand out better there.

"Eli, make a straight line with me, or they'll think we're asking for an ox!"

"Aye, aye, Stevie," Eli joked, saluting with his free hand.

All eight of the swimmers watched the plane, waiting for some kind of signal that the pilot understood. The plane soared through the sky, zooming along the valley toward the campsite, and then it got to the lake. It seemed to Lisa that the plane was almost suspended above them, though of course it was really moving quite fast. Then, as they all watched, the pilot made a traditional salute, acknowledging receipt of their message by dipping each of his wings in turn. Then he banked and switched directions, leaving the valley the same way he'd come.

"We did it!" Stevie shrieked joyously, swimming back to shore and the comfort of her towel.

"Boy, it's a good thing we weren't in trouble," Kate

remarked as she dried herself. "There aren't enough of us to spell SOS."

"Even with Amy and Seth," Lisa added.

"No problem there," Stevie said. "Those two spell SOS all by themselves!"

ONE ADVANTAGE THEY'D gained by their night journey away from the forest fire was that they had traveled a full day's distance in the dark of night and, ironically, that put them one full day ahead of schedule. In practical terms that meant that they could stay in this campsite all day long, since they didn't need to leave it until the next morning. From there it was just a few hours' ride back along the valley to Eli's friend's ranch. They could relax and play all day long, so when John announced that he had brought a couple of kites with him, they immediately formed informal teams for a kite-flying contest. They were involved in a heated, if friendly, argument about whether duration or height was more important by the time they reached the campsite. In fact, it was getting so heated, if friendly, that they almost missed hearing the approaching sounds of a helicopter. It was, as usual, Mel who brought it to their attention.

Immediately the eight swimmers ran to an open grassy area to re-form their well-practiced "OK." It didn't stop the helicopter from landing, scattering the horses away from the aircraft's loud, flapping propeller.

A distinguished-looking middle-aged man hopped out of the door of the helicopter.

"Where are my children?" the man demanded, running up to the now disassociated "OK."

There was only one person in the world it could be, only one person who would be so demanding, so insensitive to the animals he'd frightened or to the people he was being rude to.

"Amy and Seth are at the campsite," Stevie told him. Eli pointed the way. Without another word the man strode off in the direction Eli had pointed.

Seth and Amy appeared with their father just moments later, walking directly toward the helicopter. They didn't hesitate or stop to say good-bye. They just climbed aboard.

Their father, on the other hand, stopped in front of Eli and put his hands on his hips. "What kind of trip leader are you?" he demanded. "You take this group of children out into the wilderness and let them get trapped by a killer forest fire? You'll be sorry you treated my children this way, I tell you. You'll be hearing from my lawyer!"

Without waiting for a response, and everybody there was sure that Eli had one, Seth and Amy's father spun on his heels and aimed directly for the helicopter. His foot slipped on the steps, and his dignity slipped with it. Nobody laughed—at least not until after the door was closed and the helicopter began to rise from the ground.

For a fraction of a second, the thought crossed Stevie's mind that Amy and Seth should come back because their leaving meant that everybody else was going to have to do their work and take care of their horses. The thought passed quickly though, and then all Stevie felt was tremendous relief.

"Hip, hip hooray!" Lisa shouted at the top of her lungs. Everybody else joined in. Even Mel barked.

12

"Now about that kite-flying contest . . ." John brought everybody's attention away from the disappearing helicopter and back to the important issue of the day.

Although there was plenty of work to be done around the campsite, like airing out wet and smoky clothes and bedding, and sorting items that had been mashed into packs so they could be loaded quickly, to say nothing about figuring out what food was left for them to eat for the last day of the trip, there were also a lot of fun things to be done, and everybody wanted to see to it that they got done—all of them.

First, they flew kites. One snapped its string and sailed off into the sky. Stevie opined that that was definitely the highest and longest flight. Everybody else was laughing too hard to argue with her. Then they exercised their horses by riding bareback. Since Christine frequently rode bareback, she was the best at it and gave them all tips.

"It's the best way there is to feel the movement of the horse. There's no saddle between you and him, so you can tell everything with your legs. It's also easier to talk to him with your legs."

At first Lisa had some trouble with the bareback riding. She hadn't had much practice at it and found she missed the saddle for balance.

"It's a little like riding a bicycle," Carole told her. "Once you realize you have to go with the movement of the horse instead of trying to compensate for it, as you can in a saddle with stirrups, you'll do fine. You'll also do better in the saddle as a result."

Lisa tried it. First, she slipped to the right and had to hold onto Chocolate's mane to keep from slipping right off.

"It's a good thing horses don't have nerves in their manes," Stevie remarked, looking at Lisa's white knuckles clutching at the thick black hairs of the horse's mane.

"And I wish I didn't have nerves in my . . ." Lisa countered, straightening herself up.

"Oh yes, you do," Carole told her. "It's really important to feel with your seat and your legs. Just relax and let it be natural."

"Natural, natural, natural," Lisa told herself while Chocolate trotted easily in a large circle. She found that the tempo of her own voice began to match the pace of Chocolate's gait, and that her own movements, slight though they were, began to match those of the horse. It was as if she were trotting along with her.

"You're doing it!" Carole said excitedly. "I can see. You've got it!"

"I do!" Lisa agreed. "I think the secret is to let the horse do the work. I'm just along for the ride, right?"

"Right," Stevie echoed. "Nice job!"

Lisa was proud of the work she'd done, even though it mostly consisted of letting the horse do the work. Using her legs to signal Chocolate, she brought her to a walk and then a stop. She leaned forward and patted her on the neck. "Good girl," she said.

"Good girl to you," Christine added. "Next time we'll try that at a lope."

Although Lisa was pleased with her bareback trotting, she thought she'd be able to wait quite a while to try bareback loping!

LUNCH AT THE campsite was more than a little odd. It seemed that most of what they'd been able to pack up before their dash from the approaching fire was potato chips and fresh fruit. Eli and Jeannie hinted that they were saving something good for dinner, so the riders weren't too concerned about their stomachs. Besides, as the morning's fisherwomen pointed out, they'd had a magnificent breakfast.

In the afternoon they went swimming again and then took a relaxed hike through the valley. Lisa and Christine collected wildflowers. Some, they said, they were going to dry and take home. Others were selected to adorn their dinner table that evening.

"What dinner table?" Stevie asked. "We don't have a dinner table."

"Since when did you get so particular about particulars?" Lisa joked. "Don't worry, we'll find something to adorn!"

Stevie smiled and shrugged. She and Kate were chatting about competition riding. Stevie wanted to get some ideas from her about the aspects of competition that went beyond riding skills.

"So tell me about psyching out the other riders." Stevie said.

"There are a million theories," Kate replied. "They range from not speaking to any of the other riders until the competition is over, to being friendly with everybody, and everything in between. Personally, I found that the only way I could compete successfully was to be myself and to ride the best I knew how."

That, Stevie decided, was the best way to do it.

Carole and John walked together, behind the others. They, too, talked about horses. They talked about riding them, about training them, about breeding them, about owning them, and everything else about them they could think of. Carole was always happy talking about horses, and she found herself feeling particularly happy to be talking about horses with John. She was so content to be near her friends and with John, that when he took her hand and squeezed it gently, it seemed to be the most natural thing in the world. She squeezed back and smiled to herself.

"So, now, tell me more about how you're finishing Starlight's training," John said.

Carole was only too happy to do so.

*   *   *

DINNER TURNED OUT to be just as odd, and just as nice, as lunch had been. Jeannie and Eli had found a few cans of hash and a few cans of beans. They mixed them together and made a strange sort of stew.

"I think if my mother put this in front of me at home, I'd just throw it out," Stevie said.

"You don't like my cooking?" Jeannie asked, pretending to be hurt.

"No, that's not what I meant at all," Stevie told her. "Look at my plate—it's empty. I'll even have more if there is any. It tastes great to me."

"Must be the wood fire," Eli said. "That always gives everything a great taste."

"What you mean is that it makes everything smoky, so that when you make a weird mixture like hash and beans, it just tastes like smoke," Kate suggested.

"Would you like seconds, too?" Eli asked.

"You bet!" Kate told him.

When the last of the hash and beans was gone, Eli stood up in front of all his riders circling the camp fire. He began talking in his strongest, phoniest cowboy drawl.

"It's tahm fo' an ole cowpoke tradition," he said, drawing out each word slowly.

"Ghost stories?" Stevie asked eagerly.

"Nah," Eli scoffed. "It's gonna be tall tales, and s'mores."

"You mean we get to lie—and eat *real* food?"

"A-yep!" Eli confirmed.

"Bring on the marshmallows!"

The Saddle Club girls thought of themselves as being particularly good with tall tales. In fact, it was a tradition at Pine Hollow to make up stories about the owner Max Regnery's grandfather. Stevie considered herself the all-time champion, so she declared that she would go first.

She told the riders the story of the discovery of Victoria Pass—the very place they were camping.

"A long time ago there was this hunter who lived nearby. He tracked a deer through the mountains. He tracked and he tracked and he tracked it for weeks. He became obsessed with catching this deer."

"How obsessed was he?" Carole asked.

"Just wait and I'll tell you," Stevie assured her. "He reached the top of one mountain, which stood just about where we are now sitting, and for the first time he had a clear shot at the deer. He raised his rifle to his shoulder and squinted to focus, trying to get the deer into the cross hairs of his target scope—"

"I thought this took place a long time ago," John teased. "They didn't have cross hairs then."

"Shhhh," Carole said.

"But when he squinted, it made his contact lens pop out, and he couldn't see a thing with the eye he used to aim. So he dropped his rifle, and he began rummaging around in the ground under his feet. Pretty soon, when he still couldn't find the lens, he began digging, tossing dirt every which way. Before he knew it, he'd dug up the entire mountain and left us this beautiful valley."

"Did he ever find his contact lens?" Lisa asked.

"Nah, it was probably lost at the bottom of the lake."

"And the deer?" John asked.

"He stopped hunting it. He now lives exclusively on hash and beans!"

"Very good!" Eli said, clapping along with the others. He handed Stevie a s'more. "Who's next?"

"Me," Lisa said, raising her hand. "I've got one."

"Okay, let's hear it," Jeannie said.

"Once upon a time—"

"Not a fairy tale, a *tall* tale!" Christine teased.

"Don't worry; it's tall," Lisa said. Then she began again. "Once upon a time there were a brother and sister. They looked just like everybody else, and sometimes they even acted like everybody else, but they really weren't."

"I'll second that!" Stevie said. Everybody laughed, and then Lisa took a deep breath to continue.

"Lisa, you don't have to do this," Carole said. "They're gone, and it's good riddance."

"Maybe they even learned something from the experience and will change," Christine said.

"I doubt it," Lisa said. "They won't change as long as there's somebody there to pick up the pieces for them— like me, or their father."

"I thought we were telling tall tales," Eli said. Everybody knew he was trying to veer the riders away from the subject of Seth and Amy, but Lisa also felt there was something that she wanted to say.

Lisa dropped all pretense of a tall tale. "Anyway," she said. "I was pretty busy for a while there, trying to make the world right for Seth, if not for Amy. I didn't see that what was happening instead was that they were making it all wrong for me—and you guys, too. So do me a favor, will you?"

"Whatever you want," Stevie said.

"Next time I get mixed up with a pair of jerks like that, will you remind me of this not-so-tall tale?"

"Definitely!" Carole said. That was an easy promise for everyone to make.

"See, that wasn't a tall tale, that was a jerk tale," Eli complained. "Who's got another tall tale to tell?"

It seemed that almost everybody did, and much to everybody's relief, none of the rest of the stories had any serious morals.

Later, when the full moon had risen high in the black velvet sky, it was time to sleep. It was too beautiful a night to sleep in tents, so they all brought their sleeping bags out into the open and laid them in a circle around the embers of the camp fire.

It had been such a wonderful day that Stevie didn't want it to end. She wondered if she could stay awake all night and decided to do it by counting the stars overhead. Although she was sure there were thousands scattered across the vast sky, she was sound asleep before she got to seventeen.

13

TWENTY-FOUR HOURS later The Saddle Club was having its first meeting in five days. Carole, Lisa, Stevie, Kate, and Christine all sat in comfortable chairs on the porch of one of the bunkhouses at the Bar None Ranch. It had been a long day, though not nearly as long as the day and night of the fire. They had left their lakeside campsite early in the morning and ridden two hours to the horse ranch, where the vans awaited them. Jeannie and Eli had dropped the girls off at the airport so that Frank could fly them back to the Bar None. It would take Jeannie and Eli another day to return with the horse vans by highway.

Now there was only one more night of the trip before

Stevie, Lisa, and Carole had to return home. There seemed to be so much to talk about.

"I never thought a shower could feel that good," Stevie said, snuggling in her freshly washed flannel pajamas.

"There is something to be said for civilization," Lisa agreed.

"But I wouldn't trade our experience on the pack trip for anything," Carole added.

"Especially the part about holding hands with John?" Kate asked her.

"Especially that," Carole agreed.

"Are you going to write to him?" Christine asked.

"I think so," Carole said. "He lives a couple of thousand miles from me, so who knows if we'll ever see each other again? But he's smart about horses, and I like that. He wants me to keep him up-to-date on Starlight's training."

"Writing letters is nice," Stevie said.

"You mean like the four postcards you mailed to your boyfriend Phil this afternoon?" Lisa asked.

"Sure," Stevie said, shrugging and smiling, recalling all the information she'd had to jam onto four little postcards. "After all, I told him I'd send him postcards, I didn't say when I'd send them. Besides, I like to write."

"Everything but homework, right?" Carole said.

"Oh," Stevie said. It was a stilted utterance, almost a gasping sound. "Oh, no!"

"What's the matter?" Lisa asked.

"The word—*homework*. I just remembered."

"You have homework?" Carole asked.

"It's my book report," Stevie said. "I brought the book with me, don't you remember? It's *Robinson Crusoe.* Have you seen it? What happened to it?" She jumped up from the porch and ran to her bunk. She began rummaging through her clean, neatly folded belongings. There wasn't a sign of *Robinson Crusoe.* "My parents are going to kill me. I promised, absolutely positively promised, I'd have the thing written and practically typed and proofread by the time we got back."

Shirts, pajamas, socks, and underwear were flying around the cabin. "Is it in your bag?" Stevie asked Carole, sounding desperate. Carole shook her head. "I've just got to have that book!"

"Hold it!" Lisa commanded, trying to pick up the various pieces of clothing that were scattered on the floor, the bunk beds, and even draped on the ceiling light fixture. "Let's think this thing out logically."

Stevie stopped her desperate search. Lisa's specialty was logic. More than once Lisa's logic had gotten Stevie out of hot water. Maybe, just maybe, it would work again.

"You must have left the book at the campsite on the mountain when you packed up your things to get away from the fire," Kate suggested. That was the logical answer to the question, but it didn't help Stevie get the report done.

"I know about *Robinson Crusoe*," Carole said. "It's about a man who gets shipwrecked on a desert island and survives, right?"

"Yes," Stevie said. "I learned that from the back of the book. I don't think I can write a whole book report with just that information, though of course I could try."

"Forget about that," Carole said. "It'll never work. But since you're supposed to write about wilderness survival, why don't you just write the story of our wilderness ride instead? After all, we survived a forest fire! I bet your teacher will love it! What do you think, Lisa?"

Lisa furrowed her brows, obviously thinking hard. "I don't think that's necessary," she said finally. "I think if you just tell your parents and your teacher about the forest fire, they will all think it's the most original excuse you've *ever* come up with for not handing in an assignment. They're going to love it!"

"That's why I love The Saddle Club," Stevie declared. "Just when you need help, it's there for you!"

ABOUT THE AUTHOR

BONNIE BRYANT is the author of more than forty books for young readers, including novelizations of movie hits such as *Teenage Mutant Ninja Turtles* and *Honey, I Shrunk the Kids*, written under her married name, B. B. Hiller.

Ms. Bryant began writing The Saddle Club in 1986. Although she had done some riding before that, she intensified her studies then and found herself learning right along with her characters Stevie, Carole, and Lisa. She claims that they are all much better riders than she is.

Ms. Bryant was born and raised in New York City. She lives in Greenwich Village with her two sons.

T·H·E
SADDLE CLUB

A blue-ribbon series by Bonnie Bryant

Stevie, Carole and Lisa are all very different, but they *love* horses! The three girls are best friends at Pine Hollow Stables, where they ride and care for all kinds of horses. Come to Pine Hollow and get ready for all the fun and adventure that comes with being 13!

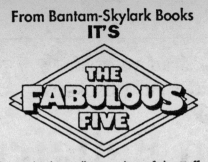

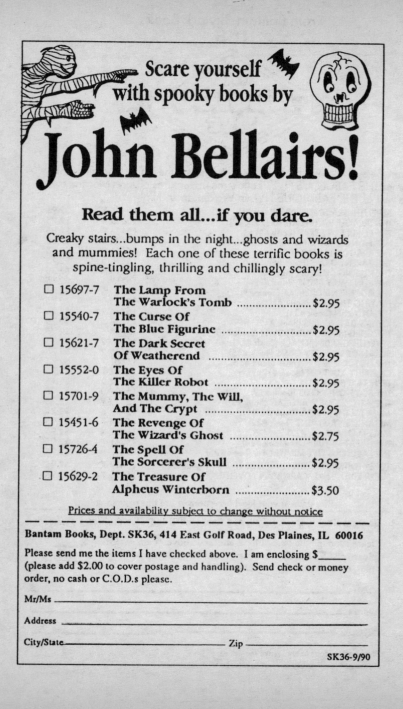